# The Canterbury Tales

## 坎特伯雷故事

商務印書館

Name of Book: The Canterbury Tales
Author: Geoffrey Chaucer
Text adaptation, notes and activities: Derek Sellen
Additional activities: Rebecca Raynes
Editors: Rebecca Raynes, Claudia Fiocco
Design and art direction: Nadia Maestri
Computer graphics: Simona Corniola
Illustrations: Giovanni Manna
Edition: ©2003 Black Cat Publishing
        an imprint of Cideb Editrice, Genoa, Canterbury

系 列 名：Black Cat 優質英語階梯閱讀 · Level 5
書　　名：坎特伯雷故事
顧　　問：Angeli Lau
責任編輯：傅　伊　葛　亮
封面設計：張　毅　曹　磊
出　　版：商務印書館（香港）有限公司
　　　　　香港筲箕灣耀興道3號東滙廣場8樓
　　　　　http://www.commercialpress.com.hk
印　　刷：中華商務彩色印刷有限公司
　　　　　香港新界大埔汀麗路36號中華商務印刷大廈
版　　次：2003年8月第1版第1次印刷
　　　　　© 2003 商務印書館（香港）有限公司
　　　　　ISBN 962 07 1660 4
　　　　　Printed in Hong Kong

# 出版說明

　　本館一向倡導優質閱讀，近年來連續推出了以 "Q" 為標識的 "Quality English Learning 優質英語學習" 系列，其中《讀名著學英語》叢書，更是香港書展入選好書，讀者反響令人鼓舞。推動社會閱讀風氣，推動英語經典閱讀，藉閱讀拓廣世界視野，提高英語水平，已經成為一種潮流。

　　然良好閱讀習慣的養成非一日之功，大多數初、中級程度的讀者，常視直接閱讀厚重的原著為畏途。如何給年輕的讀者提供切實的指引和幫助，如何既提供優質的學習素材，又提供名師的教學方法，是當下社會關注的重要問題。針對這種情況，本館特別延請香港名校名師，根據多年豐富的教學經驗，精選海外適合初、中級英語程度讀者的優質經典讀物，有系統地出版了這套叢書，名為《Black Cat 優質英語階梯閱讀》。

　　《Black Cat 優質英語階梯閱讀》體現了香港名校名師堅持經典學習的教學理念，以及多年行之有效的學習方法。既有經過改寫和縮寫的經典名著，又有富創意的現代作品；既有精心設計的聽、說、讀、寫綜合練習，又有豐富的歷史文化知識；既有彩色插圖、繪圖和照片，又有英美專業演員朗讀作品的 CD。適合口味不同的讀者享受閱讀之樂，欣賞經典之美。

　　《Black Cat 優質英語階梯閱讀》由淺入深，逐階提升，好像參與一個尋寶遊戲，入門並不難，但要真正尋得寶藏，需要投入，更需要堅持。只有置身其中的人，才能體味純正英語的魅力，領略得到真寶的快樂。當英語閱讀成為自己生活的一部分，英語水平的提高自然水到渠成。

商務印書館（香港）有限公司

編輯部

# 使用説明 _____

## 1 應該怎樣選書？

### 按閲讀興趣選書

《Black Cat 優質英語階梯閲讀》精選世界經典作品，也包括富於創意的現代作品；既有膾炙人口的小説、戲劇，又有非小説類的文化知識讀物，品種豐富，內容多樣，適合口味不同的讀者挑選自己感興趣的書，享受閲讀的樂趣。

### 按英語程度選書

《Black Cat 優質英語階梯閲讀》現設 Level 1 至 Level 6，由淺入深，涵蓋初、中級英語程度。讀物分級採用了國際上通用的劃分標準，主要以詞彙（vocabulary）和結構（structures）劃分。

Level 1 至 Level 3 出現的詞彙較淺顯，相對深的核心詞彙均配上中文解釋，節省讀者查找詞典的時間，以專心理解正文內容。在註釋的幫助下，讀者若能流暢地閲讀正文內容，就不用擔心這一本書程度過深。

Level 1 至 Level 3 出現的動詞時態形式和句子結構比較簡單。動詞時態形式以現在時（present simple）、現在時進行式（present continuous）、過去時（past simple）為主，句子結構大部分是簡單句（simple sentences）。此外，還包括比較級和最高級（comparative and superlative forms）、可數和不可數名詞（countable and uncountable nouns）以及冠詞（articles）等語法知識點。

Level 4 至 Level 6 出現的動詞時態形式，以現在完成時（present perfect）、現在完成時進行式（present perfect continuous）、過去完成時（past perfect continuous）為主，句子結構大部分是複合句（compound sentences）、條件從句（1st and 2nd conditional sentences）等。此外，還包括情態動詞（modal verbs）、被動形式（passive forms）、動名詞（gerunds）、

短語動詞（phrasal verbs）等語法知識點。

　　根據上述的語法範圍，讀者可按自己實際的英語水平，如詞彙量、語法知識、理解能力、閱讀能力等自主選擇，不再受制於學校年級劃分或學歷高低的約束，完全根據個人需要選擇合適的讀物。

## ② 怎樣提高閱讀效果？

　　閱讀的方法主要有兩種：一是泛讀，二是精讀。兩者各有功能，適當地結合使用，相輔相成，有事半功倍之效。

　　泛讀，指閱讀大量適合自己程度（可稍淺，但不能過深）、不同內容、風格、體裁的讀物，但求明白內容大意，不用花費太多時間鑽研細節，主要作用是多接觸英語，減輕對它的生疏感，鞏固以前所學過的英語，讓腦子在潛意識中吸收詞彙用法、語法結構等。

　　精讀，指小心認真地閱讀內容精彩、組織有條理、遣詞造句又正確的作品，着重點在於理解"準確"及"深入"，欣賞其精彩獨到之處。精讀時，可充分利用書中精心設計的練習，學習掌握有用的英語詞彙和語法知識。精讀後，可再花十分鐘朗讀其中一小段有趣的文字，邊唸邊細心領會文字的結構和意思。

　　《Black Cat 優質英語階梯閱讀》中的作品均值得精讀，如時間有限，不妨嘗試每兩個星期泛讀一本，輔以每星期挑選書中一章精彩的文字精讀。要學好英語，持之以恆地泛讀和精讀英文是最有效的方法。

## ③ 本系列的練習與測試有何功能？

　　《Black Cat 優質英語階梯閱讀》特別注重練習的設計，為讀者考慮周到，切合實用需求，學習功能強。每章後均配有訓練聽、說、讀、寫四項技能的練習，分量、難度恰到好處。

聽力練習分兩類，一是重聽故事回答問題，二是聆聽主角對話、書信朗讀、或模擬記者訪問後寫出答案，旨在以生活化的練習形式逐步提高聽力。每本書均配有 CD 提供作品朗讀，朗讀者都是專業演員，英國作品由英國演員錄音，美國作品由美國演員錄音，務求增加聆聽的真實感和感染力。多聆聽英式和美式英語兩種發音，可讓讀者熟悉二者的差異，逐漸培養分辨英美發音的能力，提高聆聽理解的準確度。此外，模仿錄音朗讀故事或模仿主人翁在戲劇中的對白，都是訓練口語能力的好方法。

閱讀理解練習形式多樣化，有縱橫字謎、配對、填空、字句重組等等，注重訓練讀者的理解、推敲和聯想等多種閱讀技能。

寫作練習尤具新意，教讀者使用網式圖示（spidergrams）記錄重點，採用問答、書信、電報、記者採訪等多樣化形式，鼓勵讀者動手寫作。

書後更設有升級測試（Exit Test）及答案，供讀者檢查學習效果。充分利用書中的練習和測試，可全面提升聽、說、讀、寫四項技能。

## ◆ 4 本系列還能提供甚麼幫助？

《Black Cat 優質英語階梯閱讀》提倡豐富多元的現代閱讀，巧用書中提供的資訊，有助於提升英語理解力，擴闊視野。

每本書都設有專章介紹相關的歷史文化知識，經典名著更有作者生平、社會背景等資訊。書內富有表現力的彩色插圖、繪圖和照片，使閱讀充滿趣味，部分加上如何解讀古典名畫的指導，增長見識。有的書還提供一些與主題相關的網址，比如關於不同國家的節慶源流的網址，讓讀者多利用網上資源增進知識。

# Contents

**FCE** First Certificate in English Examination-style exercises

T: GRADE 7 Trinity-style exercises (Grade 7)

This story is recorded in full. 故事錄音

This symbol indicates the chapters and activities featured on the accompanying CD. 文章和聽力練習的錄音標記

*Geoffrey Chaucer* (after 1400) by unknown artist.

# The Life of Geoffrey Chaucer

Geoffrey Chaucer is often called 'the Father of English poetry', the first great writer in English. He was born in London in about 1340, the son of John Chaucer, an important wine merchant. For most of his life, Geoffrey was connected with the royal court in London in various ways, and official records often mention his name.

When he was about sixteen, he became a page [1] in the household [2] of one of the King's daughters-in-law. In 1359, he served as a soldier in the war in France. He was taken prisoner but released for a ransom, [3] part of which the King himself paid. During the 1360's, he worked in

---

1. **page** : a boy servant.
2. **household** : all the people living together in a house.
3. **ransom** : money which is paid for the freedom of a prisoner.

the King's household and was in contact with the sophisticated [1]
society of the court. Perhaps he was responsible for entertaining the
lords and ladies with stories. He married Philippa, a lady-in-waiting [2]
to the Queen, and had at least two sons. One, Thomas Chaucer, went
on to become one of the richest men in England. Geoffrey became
closely connected to the powerful family of the Duke of Lancaster
and wrote a famous poem on the death of the Duchess.

Chaucer describes himself in his writing as a fat man with a modest,
simple personality. It seems that he was deeply interested in religion
but also enjoyed earthy [3] humour. One of his most famous characters
is the Wife of Bath, a woman who had been married five times and
had had many lovers! Many of his works are about love and
marriage, especially about the equality of men and women. At the
end of *The Canterbury Tales*, he apologises for writing some stories
which are against established [4] religion.

One of the most important events of his life was his visit to Italy in
1372. He stayed there for eleven months, visiting Genoa, Pisa and
Florence. He already knew French literature very well but now he
came into contact with the works of Dante, Boccaccio and Petrarch.
This Italian influence was very strong in his later work. The plan of
*The Canterbury Tales* – where each pilgrim [5] tells a story to the
others – is almost certainly based upon Boccaccio's *Decameron*.

He also realised the importance of creating literature in the vernacular, [6]
in the language of the people. Dante had established Italian as a
literary language; Chaucer wanted to do the same for English.

---

1. **sophisticated** : having a lot of experience of the world.
2. **lady-in-waiting** : companion.
3. **earthy** : talking about subjects which other people avoid or feel ashamed about.
4. **established** : made official for a country.
5. **pilgrim** : person who travels to a holy place as an act of religious devotion.
6. **the vernacular** : the common language of the people.

| | CHAUCER | HIS TIMES |
|---|---|---|
| 1386 | Chaucer writes *The Legend of Good Women* | |
| 1387-1392 | Chaucer begins *The Canterbury Tales* | |
| 1388 | | Richard II closest supporters are removed |
| 1391-1392 | Chaucer writes *The Treatise of the Astrolabe* | |
| 1392-1395 | Chaucer writes most of *The Canterbury Tales* | |
| June 1394 | | Death of Queen Anne |
| 1396 | | Richard II marries princess Isabel, daughter of king Philip of VI of France to bring an end to the wars |
| 1396-1400 | Chaucer writes the latest of *The Canterbury Tales* | |
| 1400 | Chaucer writes *The Complaint of Chaucer to His Purse* | |
| 25 October 1400 | Chaucer's death | |

# INTERNET PROJECT

Read the chronology about Chaucer's times on the web. You may research the following topics:

▶ The Hundred Years' War
▶ The English monarchy
▶ Italian poets

# Summary

1t is the middle of the fourteenth century. A group of pilgrims are travelling from the Tabard Inn in London to the shrine [1] of Thomas Becket in Canterbury. On the way, they decide that each traveller should tell a story – about love, about marriage, about war, about murder, about jealousy, about magic. The Knight tells a tale of high romance. [2] The Pardoner tells a story of death. And the Wife of Bath tells the story of her life, of her five husbands and her fight to control the men in her life. But The Tales end with the story of the perfect marriage and how, if we are generous to one another, we can find the perfect society.

## Before you begin

**1** **Think about these questions:**

   **a.** How much have people changed in the last six hundred years?
   **b.** Is friendship more important than love?
   **c.** Do dreams have a meaning?
   **d.** Will men do anything for gold?
   **e.** What do women most desire?
   **f.** What makes a perfect marriage?

**As you read the six parts of *The Canterbury Tales*, you will find some answers!**

---

1. **shrine** : a special place where people come to worship.
2. **high romance** : love affairs of the upper classes.

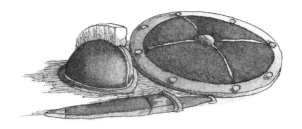

# PART ONE

# The Prologue

n April, when the sweet showers [1] fall and feed the roots in the earth, the flowers begin to bloom. [2] The soft wind blows from the west and the young sun rises in the sky. The small birds sing in the green forests. Then people want to go on pilgrimages. From every part of England, they go to Canterbury to visit the tomb of Thomas Becket, the martyr, [3] who helped the sick.

My name is Geoffrey Chaucer. People say that I am a poet but I am not really very important. I am just a story-teller. One day in spring, I was staying in London at the Tabard Inn. [4] At night, a

---

1. **showers** : light rain.
2. **bloom** : come into flower.
3. **martyr** : person who is killed or made to suffer greatly because of his religious or political beliefs.
4. **the Tabard Inn** : the name of the pub where Chaucer and the pilgrims stayed. A 'tabard' was a soldier's jacket.

great crowd of people arrived at the inn, ready to go on a pilgrimage to Canterbury. I soon made friends with them and promised to join them.

'You must get up early,' they told me. 'We are leaving when the sun rises.'

Before I begin my story, I will describe the pilgrims to you. There were twenty-nine. There were men and women, young and old, fat and thin, ugly and beautiful, poor men and lords, some riding, some walking, some who lived good lives, others who were bad. If you want to know about the world of human beings, then go on a pilgrimage!

First of all, there was a knight. He was a brave man who had fought for chivalry, [1] truth and honour. He had taken part in wars in all parts of the world. He always fought bravely and he always killed his enemy. Although he was a famous man, he was modest, sincere and polite. He was a perfect gentleman.

The Knight rode a fine horse but his clothes still carried the marks of war. He was going on the pilgrimage to thank God for his victories.

The Knight's son, a fine young Squire, [2] rode with him. He was twenty years old, with curly [3] hair and a handsome face. He had fought well in war to win the love of his lady. He knew how to ride well, to write songs and poems, to draw and to dance. The girls all loved him, that handsome young man.

---

1. **chivalry** : courtesy and concern for the weak and the helpless.
2. **squire** : a young man who served a knight.
3. **curly** : not straight.

# The Canterbury Tales

There was a countryman riding with him. He carried a bow and arrows, a sword and a hunting horn. His face was brown and his clothes were green. There were peacock feathers on his arrows. He was a true man of the forest.

Then there was an elegant Prioress. Her name was Madam Eglantine. She spoke fine French with an English accent and had very good manners. When she was eating, she was careful not to make a mess. [1] What a fine, sensitive lady! If she saw a mouse which was caught in a trap, [2] she cried. She gave roast meat or milk or fine white bread to her little dogs and, if one died, she was sad for weeks.

She had grey eyes, small soft red lips and a wide forehead. Her clothes were fashionable. She wore a graceful cloak, a coral bracelet, [3] some beads and a golden brooch [4] marked with an 'A'. 'Amor vincit omnia' was written on it. That is Latin – 'Love conquers all'.

There was another nun, a secretary and three priests. Also, there was a fat monk who wore rich clothes and loved hunting. His favourite food was roast swan. [5] Next to him, there was a merry Friar. This fat Friar loved pretty girls, silver and gold and singing. He knew all the inns in town and loved drinking better than praying.

---

1. **make a mess** : make something untidy, disordered or dirty.
2. **trap** : a thing to catch animals, e.g. mice.
3. **bracelet** : a band worn around your wrist or arm as a decoration.
4. **brooch** : a piece of jewellery that you fasten to your clothes.
5. **swan** : a beautiful white bird.

# The Prologue

These were all religious people. But they loved the world – a
fashionable lady, a rich monk and a pleasure-loving friar!

All kinds of people rode on the pilgrimage. There was a rich
Merchant with a long beard and rich clothes. He knew how to
make money and rode a fat horse. But next to him, the Oxford
Cleric [1] rode a thin horse. He preferred to have books by great
philosophers next to his bed, not bags of money. A Franklin [2]
with a white beard rode with them, a man who loved good food
and wine.

After them, there was a Cook who knew how to cook delicious
meals with herbs and spices. [3] Then there was a brown-faced Sea-
Captain who looked like a pirate. He had fought battles at sea and
made his prisoners walk the plank. [4] Then there was a doctor who
knew everything about the body. His patients paid him with gold.
The plague had made him very rich indeed!

Look at the next pilgrim! She was a large red-faced woman
from the city of Bath. She wore a huge hat and a long coat over
her wide hips. [5] Her tights [6] were red and her shoes were new. Her
face was as red as her clothes. How many husbands do you think
she had been married to? Five! She had lived longer than them
all. That is how she became rich enough to go on pilgrimages, to
Jerusalem, to Spain, to France, to Rome... The Wife of Bath liked

---

1. **cleric** : religious scholar.
2. **franklin** : land-owner.
3. **herbs and spices** : natural substances to add flavour to food.
4. **plank** : a long piece of wood. Pirates made their enemies walk off the ship
   and fall into the sea.
5. **hips** : the widest part of the body.
6. **tights** : covering for the legs.

to laugh and talk about love, a subject in which she was an expert! What a woman!

Now, I will tell you about the Miller. [1] He was a great, fat, strong man with a red beard and huge muscles. On the end of his large red nose, there was a large red hairy wart. [2] The Miller loved drinking and telling jokes. But he was an expert thief who stole corn from his customers. As the pilgrims rode out of town, the Miller played the bagpipes. [3] Everyone knew that we were coming!

A Parson was also travelling with us. He loved God and loved to help other people. He gave money to the poor, gave advice to people with problems and visited the sick, even when the weather was bad. He was a very good man.

But behind him, I am sorry to tell you, there were two bad men. One was a Summoner. His job was to punish people who broke the religious laws. The church was very strong in those times, so he had a lot of power. And he used it to make money from poor people who were afraid of him. This Summoner had a red face with large pimples. [4] He stank [5] of garlic and onions. [6] He looked so terrible that children were afraid when they saw him!

The other man was the Pardoner. He had long yellow hair like rats' tails with no beard. Uggh! If people gave him money, he forgave them in the name of the Church. That was his job. He always carried bits of wood and cloth and bones which he said

---

1. **miller** : a man who made wheat into flour.
2. **wart** : a hard dry growth on the skin.
3. **bagpipes** : a musical instrument.
4. **pimples** : red spots on the face.
5. **stank** : had a very unpleasant and offensive smell.
6. **garlic and onions** : strong-smelling things to eat.

# The Prologue

came from the Virgin Mary or Jesus or the saints. He was a liar, of course. He earned far more money than the honest Parson. When he sang in church, he had a fine voice. But his heart was black and ugly.

There were many other pilgrims. But it will be boring if I tell you about them all. It's time to begin telling the stories.

I shall tell you everything about the pilgrimage. But please remember that I am only repeating what the pilgrims said and did. If sometimes the stories which they told are not polite, it's not my fault. [1] I must tell the truth, mustn't I?

The pilgrims began their journey from the Tabard Inn on the south bank of the Thames. Before we left, the Host [2] gave us all a great meal. After we had eaten, he spoke to us. He was a large, bright-eyed man who loved to have fun.

'Welcome, ladies and gentlemen. I have decided to come with you to visit Saint Thomas. I hope we all enjoy our journey to Canterbury. I have an idea which will help us to enjoy the long pilgrimage. Each person must tell a story on the way to Canterbury. And another story on the way back! We'll give a prize to the person who tells the best story. What do you think?'

All the pilgrims agreed with this idea. They ordered more wine and then went to bed. Early next morning, the Host woke everybody up.

'Who will tell the first story?' he asked. 'I choose the Knight.'

'Very well,' said the Knight. 'I will begin the game. Let's start riding towards Canterbury – and listen to my story.'

---

1. **fault** : responsibility.
2. **host** : the owner of the inn.

# Comprehension and Opinion

**1** **What did Chaucer tell us in The Prologue?**

    **a.** When and where did Chaucer meet the pilgrims?

    **b.** Why did the girls like the Squire?

    **c.** Did the Prioress like animals?

    **d.** What was the Wife of Bath wearing?

    **e.** Did the Summoner and the Pardoner care about religion?

    **f.** What was the Host's idea?

**2** **What do you think?**

Which pilgrims did Chaucer admire?

Which pilgrims did Chaucer dislike?

Are there people in our society who are like Chaucer's pilgrims?

# Appearance

**3** Chaucer describes the Prioress.
He writes about her cloak, her
beads, her bracelet and her
brooch. Can you label these on
the picture?

26

Here is a list of 30 words:

> attractive    beard    blonde    blouse    bracelet    brooch
> cloak    curly    ear-rings    elegant    elbow    finger
> graceful    hat    handsome    hips    jacket    knee
> moustache    necklace    overcoat    pendant [1]    pretty
> ring    straight    skirt    thumb    ugly    wavy    wrist

Divide them into five lists of six words each.

| Jewellery | Hair | Clothes | Appearance | Parts of the body |
|-----------|------|---------|------------|-------------------|
|           |      |         |            |                   |
|           |      |         |            |                   |
|           |      |         |            |                   |

## Spot the Difference

**4** Here is the beginning of The Prologue. But listen carefully there are ten changes. Listen once. Pause to take notes. Listen again. Write down as many differences as you can spot.

Differences:

1. ................................................ 2. ................................................
3. ................................................ 4. ................................................
5. ................................................ 6. ................................................
7. ................................................ 8. ................................................
9. ................................................ 10. ................................................

If necessary listen for a third time, following the text on pages 19-20. How many differences can you spot?

---

1.  **pendant** : an ornament that you wear on a chain around your neck.

T: GRADE 7

**5** **Topic – Clothes**
**Collect some recent pictures / photos of people of different ages from your country.**
**Talk about the pictures:**

1. Compare the clothes in the pictures to those in this book.

2. Say what women were not allowed to wear in the past in your country.

3. Say what visitors to your country would see / not see people wearing.

................................................................................................................
................................................................................................................
................................................................................................................
................................................................................................................
................................................................................................................
................................................................................................................
................................................................................................................
................................................................................................................

## Relative Pronouns

We can use these words **who, which, whose, where** to link sentences. For example:

The Miller bought wheat. He turned the wheat into flour.
The Miller bought wheat *which* he turned into flour.

The Prioress was the leader of the Priory. The nuns lived there.
The Prioress was the leader of the Priory *where* the nuns lived.

The Knight had fought in many wars. He was famous.
The Knight, *who* had fought in many wars, was famous.

**6** **Now match sentences 1-8 with sentences a-h.**

1. $\boxed{e}$  Canterbury is a city in Kent.
2. $\boxed{\phantom{x}}$  The Wife of Bath had been married five times.
3. $\boxed{\phantom{x}}$  Chaucer wrote *The Canterbury Tales*.
4. $\boxed{\phantom{x}}$  Pilgrimages usually begin in April.
5. $\boxed{\phantom{x}}$  The Prioress had several little dogs.
6. $\boxed{\phantom{x}}$  The Pardoner and the Summoner were bad men.
7. $\boxed{\phantom{x}}$  Chaucer stayed at the Tabard Inn.
8. $\boxed{\phantom{x}}$  The Knight was a perfect gentleman.

a. The pilgrims started their journey at the Tabard Inn.
b. She was an expert in love.
c. April is the first month of spring.
d. They took money from the poor.
e. Thomas Becket died there.
f. His son was loved by all the girls.
g. She loved them.
h. He lived in the fourteenth century.

**Now make each pair of sentences into one sentence by using *who* (for people) or *which* (for things) or *whose* (for possession) or *where* (for place).**

..............................................................................................
..............................................................................................
..............................................................................................
..............................................................................................
..............................................................................................
..............................................................................................
..............................................................................................
..............................................................................................

**FCE 7** Look at Part One and for each question below choose from the people (A-K). The people may be chosen more than once. When more than one answer is required, these may be given in any order. There is an example at the beginning (0).

| | | | |
|---|---|---|---|
| **A** | the Countryman | **B** | the Knight |
| **C** | the Friar | **D** | Geoffrey Chaucer |
| **E** | the Prioress | **F** | the Squire |
| **G** | the Monk | **H** | the Summoner |
| **I** | the Wife of Bath | **J** | the Pardoner |
| **K** | the Merchant | | |

**Which person(s):**

was staying at the Tabard Inn?  **0.** $\boxed{D}$

was sincere, polite and modest?  **1.** ☐

had fought in war for love?  **2.** ☐

was a true man of the forest?  **3.** ☐

spoke French?  **4.** ☐

loved pretty girls and drinking?  **5.** ☐

loved the world?  **6.** ☐

loved eating roast swan?  **7.** ☐

loved singing?  **8.** ☐

had been married five times?  **9.** ☐

were bad men?  **10.** ☐  **11.** ☐

were rich?  **12.** ☐  **13.** ☐  **14.** ☐

# The New York Tales

**8** **Chaucer described the typical people of his society. Can you do the same for our century? For example:**

Imagine a group of modern travellers at an airport. They are all flying to New York. The flight is late and they are all together.

- The Fashion Model was tall and slim. She wore beautiful clothes. She sat in the airport restaurant. She was eating salad and drinking mineral water. She told us about her fashion shows in Paris, London and Milan. 'I am the star,' she said. Every five minutes, she took her bag and looked in a small silver mirror. 'I am so beautiful,' she said.

- The Businessman was eating a large steak and drinking whisky. He was fat and bald with a large red face. He carried a black case full of documents. He told us about his business meetings in all the important cities of the world. He looked at his gold Swiss watch every five minutes. 'Time is money,' he repeated.

**Write a few sentences about the other travellers.**

a. What were their jobs? Actor? Politician? Robber? Professor? Film Director? Singer? Scientist? TV star?

b. What did they look like?

c. What did they eat?

d. What did they have with them?

e. What did they talk about?

f. What did they do?

g. What did they say?

# PART TWO

# The Knight's Tale

alamon and Arcite were two cousins who lived in the Greek city of Thebes. The King of Thebes, Creon, was an old, wicked [1] man who treated his enemies very badly. Theseus, the Duke of Athens, met a group of women as he was travelling. They were crying.

'Help us, Lord Theseus. We are all widows. Creon has murdered our husbands!'

Theseus decided to attack Thebes. He sent his wife, Hippolyta, and her sister, Emily, to his palace where they would be safe. Then he marched towards Thebes with his soldiers.

Palamon and Arcite fought bravely to defend their city but, in the end, they fell unconscious [2] to the ground. The victorious

---

1. **wicked** : very bad.
2. **unconscious** : without feeling anything.

# The Knight's Tale

soldiers of Athens walked among the dead bodies on the battlefield. [1]

'Come here!' shouted a soldier. 'These two are still breathing. They're alive!'

It was Palamon and Arcite. Theseus took the two young men prisoner. He took them back to Athens and locked them in a tall dark tower. No gold could buy their freedom. They were prisoners for life!

One morning in May, Emily, the sister of Queen Hippolyta, was walking in the garden near the tower. She was as beautiful as the lilies [2] and roses that grew there. She sang like an angel. Palamon, who was looking sadly out of the window, cried out when he saw her. An arrow had gone through his heart. He had fallen in love.

Arcite heard him shout. He also came to the window and looked out through the thick iron bars. As soon as he saw Emily, he also lost his heart to her. They were both in love with the same woman!

Palamon was angry with Arcite. 'You are my friend and my cousin. When we were children, we promised that we would always help each other. Now you have betrayed [3] me! You are in love with my lady!'

---

1. **battlefield** : the place where a battle takes place.
2. **lilies** : beautiful white flowers.
3. **betrayed** : broken your promise.

'I love her more than you,' replied Arcite. 'I am right to love her. There is no law in love. But let's stop quarrelling. We are both prisoners. She will never marry either of us.'

Every day the two cousins, with burning hearts, looked through the bars and watched her walking in the garden.

Shortly after this, a duke from Thebes came to visit Duke Theseus. This visitor was a friend of Arcite and begged Theseus to release him from prison. 'I will pay you money,' he said.

Duke Theseus spoke sternly. 'I agree to let him go. But there is one condition. Arcite must leave Athens immediately. If he ever returns, he will die!'

So Arcite received his freedom but had to return to Thebes while Palamon remained in the tower all alone.

Arcite was very unhappy. 'I am free but I cannot see the lovely Emily. Palamon is far luckier than I am. Every day, he can look out of his window and watch her walking in the garden. He is in Paradise!' [1]

Palamon was equally unhappy. 'Arcite is far luckier than I am. He can collect a great army in Thebes and march against Athens. If he wins the war against Theseus, he can marry Emily. He is in Paradise!'

Arcite, however, had a different plan. He came back secretly to Athens. He looked pale and sick because he had been for so long from a broken heart. Nobody recognised him. He took off his lord's clothes and put on the clothes of a poor man. Then he went to the house of Lady Emily.

'My name is Philostrate,' he told the servants. 'I am looking for a job.'

---

1. **paradise** : a perfect place.

He was a strong, hard-working young man, so he was given a job. Arcite became the personal servant of Lady Emily! But if anyone recognised him, he would die.

Palamon was in the tower for seven years. One day, however, a friend helped him to escape. He gave the guard a glass of wine with drugs in it that made him sleep. Then Palamon ran away. He crept [1] through Athens in the middle of the night and reached the countryside where he hid in a grove. [2] Both lovers were now free.

It was May. All the fields were green, the flowers were brightly coloured and the birds were singing. Thinking about his love for Emily, Arcite rode into the countryside.

'I am in a terrible situation,' he said aloud, thinking that no-one was listening. 'I cannot use my real name. I am only a servant to the lady that I want to make my wife.'

Palamon was hiding nearby in the forest. When he heard Arcite, he was very angry and rushed towards him.

'Emily is mine!' he shouted. 'You must not love her.'

'You are a lunatic [3] for love,' said Arcite.

The two cousins began fighting, like a lion and a tiger in the forest, until they were standing in a river of blood.

On the same day, Theseus woke up early in his palace in the city. 'It is a clear bright day. We will go hunting,' he decided. He rode out into the countryside with Hippolyta, his lovely queen, and her sister, Emily. Suddenly, he saw two men fighting like animals in the middle of the forest.

'Stop!' he shouted. 'Who are you?'

---

1. **crept** : *(creep/crept/crept)* moved quietly and secretly.
2. **grove** : a small group of trees, part of a forest.
3. **lunatic** : insane person.

# The Knight's Tale

'I am Palamon,' replied one. 'I deserve to die. I have escaped from your prison. But this is Arcite. He also deserves [1] to die. He has returned to Athens from Thebes under the name of Philostrate. We are fighting because we both love the lady Emily. Kill us both at the same time!'

'Yes, you deserve to die,' said Theseus. 'You are the enemies of Athens.'

But Emily and her ladies begged Theseus not to kill them. 'They are young, handsome men from good families. Forgive them.'

Theseus thought carefully. 'A good king must not be angry. He must be calm and wise. The God of Love is very powerful. Instead of escaping to Thebes, Palamon and Arcite stayed here because they loved you, Emily, even though you didn't know anything about their love! I was a lover when I was young. I have also done stupid things for love. I will let them live.'

He turned to Palamon and Arcite. 'Only one of you can marry my sister-in-law. Go away and collect a hundred knights each. In a year's time, return to Athens. Your two armies will fight and the winner will be the husband of Emily.'

The two cousins were very happy. They knelt in front of Theseus and thanked him. Then they returned as quickly as possible to Thebes. A year later, they came back to Athens. Each rode at the head of a hundred knights. The people of Athens came out into the streets to watch.

Arcite prayed to Mars, the god of war, and Palamon prayed for the help of Venus, the goddess of love. Arcite's men carried the red flag of Mars and Palamon's men carried the white flag of Venus.

---

1. **deserves** : earns punishment for something you have done.

# The Canterbury Tales

The fighting lasted from morning until night but finally Arcite and his hundred knights gained the victory. Mars had won! 'Arcite will marry Emily,' announced Theseus.

In Heaven, among the gods and goddesses, Venus was very angry. 'I am the Queen of Love but I have lost.'

She looked down on the world and saw Arcite riding on his horse towards Emily to take her as his wife. They looked softly at each other. Women usually love the winner. But then Venus acted. Suddenly, there was an earth tremor. 1 The ground shook under Arcite's horse. The horse was frightened and threw Arcite to the ground. He fell from his saddle 2 and was badly injured.

They carried Arcite to his bed and sent for doctors. 'Emily! Emily!' he called. The doctors tried to save him but he knew that he would die. Palamon and Emily came to his bedside.

'Oh Lady Emily, I love you greatly. You are my heart's queen. Take me in your arms and listen to me carefully. I am sorry now that I quarrelled with Palamon, who loves you too. After I die, if you wish to marry, think of him.'

He looked into Emily's eyes. Then he died.

There was a great funeral. Arcite's body was placed in a great fire just as, in his life, he had burnt in the fire of love.

Emily and Palamon were both very sad. They had lost a husband, a cousin and a friend.

'Out of two sorrows, make one perfect joy,' said Theseus. 'Marry each other, as Arcite wished.'

So Emily and Palamon got married and lived all the rest of their lives in great happiness.

'And that is the end of my tale,' said the Knight.

---

1. **earth tremor** : a shaking of the land, a small earthquake.
2. **saddle** : seat for a rider on a horse.

# Comprehension and Opinion

**1** **What happened in The Knight's Tale?**

    **a.** Where did Theseus put Palamon and Arcite?

    **b.** Why did Palamon and Arcite quarrel?

    **c.** Why did Arcite return to Athens?

    **d.** What did the cousins do in the forest?

    **e.** How many knights came to the battle?

    **f.** Who won the battle? Who married Emily?

**2** **What do you think?**

Is friendship more important than love?

Arcite said: 'There is no law in love.' Do you agree?

Did Theseus do the right thing?

## Proverbs

Proverbs are traditional sayings. Arcite said:
*'There is no law in love.'*
Today we still say: *'All is fair in love and war.'*

**3** **Here are some more common proverbs. Do you understand them? Try and find a similar proverb in your own language.**

    **a.** Too many cooks spoil the broth (soup).

    **b.** A bird in the hand is worth two in the bush (a small tree).

    **c.** Many hands make light work.

    **d.** It's no use crying over spilt milk.

    **e.** People who live in glass houses shouldn't throw stones.

    **f.** One swallow (a bird that arrives in England in spring) doesn't make a summer.

# A Proverb about Love

**4** **Here is another English proverb. Each number represents a letter of the alphabet.**

1.2.'3.   4.5.2.2.5.6.   2.7.   8.9.10.5.     11.7.10.5.12.

9.13.12.    11.7.3.2.    2.8.9.13.    13.5.10.5.6.    2.7.

8.9.10.5.    11.7.10.5.12.    9.2.    9.11.11.

**If you can find the words below, you will be able to find the proverb. All the words are connected with fighting.**

|   |   |   |
|---|---|---|
| **a.** | A sport which needs big gloves: | 4. 7. **X** 1. 13. **G** |
| **b.** | Another sport where you fight: | **W** 6. 5. 3. 2. 11. 1. 13. **G** |
| **c.** | The winner: | **C.** 8. 9. **M P** 1. 7. 13. |
| **d.** | The winning side can celebrate this: | 10. 1. **C** 2. 7. 6. **Y** |
| **e.** | The opposite of this is: | 12. 5. **F** 5. 9. 2. |
| **f.** | Guns, knives, swords are all: | **W** 5. 9. **P** 7. 13. 3. |
| **g.** | Waterloo was a very important... | 4. 9. 2. 2. 11. 5. |
| **h.** | An agreement to end a war: | 2. 6. 5. 9. 2. **Y** |
| **i.** | These people fight on the land: | 2. 8. 5.    9. 6. **M Y** |
| **j.** | These people fight on the sea: | 2. 8. 5.    13. 9. 10. **Y** |
| **k.** | These people fight in the sky: | 2. 8. 5.    9. 1. 6.    **F** 7. 6. **C** 5. |
| **l.** | In a war, the opposite side is the... | 5. 13. 5. **M Y** |
| **m.** | A football team must have a good... | 9. 2. 2. 9. **C K** |
| **n.** | They also need a good... | 12. 5. **F** 5. 13. **C** 5. |
| **o.** | The opposite of 'war': | **P** 5. 9. **C** 5. |
| **p.** | The Knight is a... | 3. 7. 11. 12. 1. 5. 6. |

**Write the proverb here:**

__ __ ' __   __ __ __ __ __ __   __ __   __ __ __ __   __ __ __ __ __   __ __ __    __ __ __ __   __ __ __ __

__ __ __ __ __   __ __   __ __ __ __   __ __ __ __ __   __ __   __ __ __

**Do you understand the proverb? Both Arcite and Palamon loved – but it's difficult to say who won and who lost in the end.**

# The Miller's Tale

**FCE** **5** **You will hear the Knight's Tale and part of the Miller's Tale. For questions 1-10, tick (✓) the correct boxes true (T) or false (F).**

|  |  | T | F |
|---|---|---|---|
| **1.** | The carpenter [1] was a clever man. | ☐ | ☐ |
| **2.** | Nicholas was a lodger [2] in the house. | ☐ | ☐ |
| **3.** | Nicholas had a dream about a flood. | ☐ | ☐ |
| **4.** | He told the carpenter about his 'dream'. | ☐ | ☐ |
| **5.** | Alison drowned in the flood. | ☐ | ☐ |
| **6.** | The carpenter made three large boats. | ☐ | ☐ |
| **7.** | He put the boats in the roof. | ☐ | ☐ |
| **8.** | They all slept inside the boats. | ☐ | ☐ |
| **9.** | It rained for several weeks. | ☐ | ☐ |
| **10.** | Nicholas's trick was successful. | ☐ | ☐ |

**'All is fair in love and war.' Were Nicholas and Alison right to trick the carpenter?**

...................................................................................................

...................................................................................................

...................................................................................................

---

1.  **carpenter** : man who works with wood.
2.  **lodger** : someone who pays to stay in another person's home.

**Read the summary below and think of the word which best fits each space. Use only one word in each space. There is an example at the beginning (0).**

Palamon and Arcite were two cousins **0** ....*who*............... lived in the Greek city of Thebes. When Theseus, **1** ......................... Duke of Athens attacked their city, Palamon and Arcite fought bravely but in the **2** ......................... they were taken prisoner, taken back to Athens and locked in a tower.

One day Emily, the sister of Hippolyta, Thesues's wife, **3** ......................... walking in the garden near the tower. She was very beautiful and when Palamon and Arcite saw her they **4** ......................... fell in love with her and began arguing about who should marry her.

Soon after, Arcite was freed **5** ......................... condition that he left Athens. However, he came **6** ......................... secretly to Athens and found a job in Emily's house. After seven years Palamon escaped **7** ......................... the tower and arrived in the countryside. There he met Arcite who was out riding. The two cousins began fighting for Emily until Theseus arrived **8** ......................... Hippolyta and Emily. **9** ......................... first Thesues was very angry but then he told Palamon and Arcite to go away and collect 100 knights each and then return to Athens to fight. The winner would then marry Emily. Arcite won the **10** ......................... but as he approached Emily, he was thrown from **11** ......................... horse. As he lay dying he told Palamon and Emily to **12** ......................... married. They **13** ......................... very sad, but after the funeral they got married and lived happily together.

# The Prison Diary

**FCE 7** Imagine that you are Palamon locked in the tower and that you have managed to smuggle out a letter to a friend. Include the following points and write your letter in 120-180 words in an appropriate style.

Mention:
- seeing Emily
- the quarrel with Arcite
- Arcite's release
- the lonely years
- the plan to escape

..................................................................................................

..................................................................................................

..................................................................................................

..................................................................................................

..................................................................................................

..................................................................................................

..................................................................................................

..................................................................................................

..................................................................................................

..................................................................................................

..................................................................................................

..................................................................................................

..................................................................................................

# Thomas Becket

T homas Becket was murdered on 29th December, 1170, in Canterbury Cathedral. This was the end of Becket's life but the beginning of the great tradition of pilgrimage to Canterbury which Chaucer writes about in *The Canterbury Tales*. There are many other pieces of literature connected with Becket,

including the twentieth century play *Murder in the Cathedral* by T. S. Eliot.

Becket was born in 1118 in London. As a child, he showed 'quick understanding' and received a good education. He began a career in the Church as an administrator [1] but, in 1154, he became Chancellor [2] to King Henry II. This was one of the most powerful and important jobs in the kingdom. King Henry

*Henry II* (1133-1189) from Matthew Paris's Chronicles.

---

1. **administrator** : person responsible for managing affairs.
2. **Chancellor** : head of government in a country.

was twenty-one years old and became great friends with Thomas. For that reason, he appointed him as Archbishop of Canterbury, the head of the Church in all England, in 1162.

But Becket changed. Instead of supporting the King, he defended the power of the Church. There was a long period of disagreement between Henry and Thomas. Finally, Henry became so angry that Becket escaped to France where he stayed for six years. In 1170, he returned to England. The people of Canterbury welcomed him back to the city and he became a popular hero. He continued to attack the power of the King.

When Henry, who was in France, heard of Thomas's activities, he said angrily: 'Who will rid me of this turbulent [1] priest?' Four knights immediately set off for England. They arrived in Canterbury and looked for Thomas. His monks begged him to lock himself in the cathedral but Becket said that the house of God must remain open. The knights entered the cathedral and killed the Archbishop, with axe [2] and sword.

After the murder, King Henry showed his sorrow by coming to Canterbury. He walked barefoot through the city and was whipped by the monks. He was the first pilgrim to Canterbury. After this, pilgrims came from all over England and from other parts of Europe to visit the tomb of Becket. The Pope made him a saint and his tomb was placed at the east end of the cathedral, decorated with jewels. There were many stories of miracles, of sick people who were made well and even of dead people who came alive again because of the power of Saint Thomas.

---

1. **turbulent** : trouble-making.
2. **axe** : a sharp instrument or weapon.

Finally, however, in the time of King Henry VIII, when England changed from a Roman Catholic country to a Protestant [1] one, Becket's shrine was destroyed. Henry took all the wealth of the monks of Canterbury for the state. Today, you can still see the place where Becket was murdered. The stories of his miracles are shown in the ancient stained-glass windows [2] and there is one famous

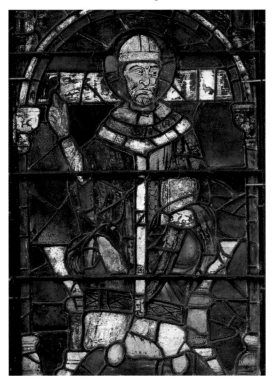

window which shows a portrait of Becket himself. Nobody, however, has ever found his bones. People believe they are buried somewhere in the cathedral. If you come to visit Canterbury, perhaps you will find them.

St Thomas à Becket shown in a stained-glass window in Canterbury Cathedral (c. 1220).

---

1. **protestant** : of any of the Christian bodies that separated from the Church of Rome in the 16th century.
2. **stained-glass windows** : windows with pictures of coloured glass.

**1** Read the story of Thomas Becket again. Then tick (✓) the correct statements true (T) or false (F). Correct the false ones.

|  | T | F |
|---|---|---|
| **a.** Becket quarrelled with Henry while he was Chancellor. | ☐ | ☐ |
| **b.** Becket supported the Church when he was Archbishop. | ☐ | ☐ |
| **c.** He was killed in the same year that he returned from France. | ☐ | ☐ |
| **d.** Henry II punished the monks for Thomas's death. | ☐ | ☐ |
| **e.** If you come to Canterbury, you can see Becket's bones. | ☐ | ☐ |

**2** Can you answer these questions without looking back?

**a.** What play did T.S. Eliot write?

**b.** When did Becket become Archbishop of Canterbury?

**c.** What words did Henry use about Becket?

**d.** How many knights came to Canterbury?

**e.** What did Henry wear on his feet when he came to Canterbury?

**f.** Where can you see pictures of Becket's miracles?

T: GRADE 7

**3** Topic – National customs

Choose an article or a picture of a typical national custom/ celebration in your country. Use it to talk about:

**1.** How you should behave during this event. What the article or picture tells/shows us about how we should behave during the event.

**2.** What visitors have to eat if they were invited. What a visitor would hear and see if they were invited. What a visitor should wear if they were invited.

**3.** How and why it is performed/celebrated.

48

✠ PART THREE ✠

# The Nun's Priest's Tale

'We need a happy tale,' said the Host, 'something to make us laugh.' He saw the Nun's Priest hiding in the background. 'Come, sir, tell us a tale. Your horse is thin and sick but I'm sure that you can tell a good story.'

'I will try to please you,' said the Priest. 'Now listen to my tale...'

Many years ago, in the magic time when all the birds and animals could speak and sing – or so I've heard – there was a poor widow who lived with her two daughters. She had three pigs, three cows and a sheep. She was a simple patient woman who worked hard and thanked God each day.

49

# The Canterbury Tales

In her farmyard, she kept a cock called Chantecleer. He was well-known in the neighbourhood. His crowing [1] was more regular than a clock or a church bell. He was a very handsome bird. He had a red comb [2] on his head, a shining black beak, [3] blue legs and golden feathers which shone [4] like fire. He was the best and proudest cockerel that has ever lived.

There were seven hens in the yard with Chantecleer. The prettiest was called Lady Pertelot. She was polite, friendly and wise. She had loved Chantecleer since she was a seven-day-old chick and she was his favourite wife. When the sun rose in the morning, the two birds sang a love-song together. It was a golden time!

But one day, while he was sleeping in the middle of his seven wives, just before the sun rose, Chantecleer began to scream.

'Darling husband,' Pertelot said, 'what's the matter?'

'Madam,' he replied, 'I have had a terrible dream. I dreamt that a horrible monster wanted to catch me and eat me. He was

---

1. **crowing** : making the sound of a cockerel, 'Cock-a-doodle-doo!'
2. **comb** : red fleshy growth on the head of a cock.
3. **beak** : hard horny part of a bird's mouth.
4. **shone** : *(shine/shone/shone)* gave bright light.

# The Nun's Priest's Tale

between yellow and red in colour. There were black tips [1] on his ears and tail. His bright eyes were fixed on me. His rows of teeth were sharp and white.'

'Don't be so afraid,' said Pertelot. 'You have lost my love. I cannot love a coward. [2] All women want strong, independent husbands, not cowards who are afraid of dreams.'

'But the dream is from God,' said Chantecleer.

'Nonsense. Dreams are nothing. All the best writers from the old times agree with me,' said the hen. 'Dreams are the result of eating too much late at night. That is all. Go to the chemist [3] and get some medicine for your stomach. I'll find you some delicious, fresh worms [4] to eat. Swallow [5] them alive! After a day or two, you will have no more bad dreams. Trust your wife, dear Chantecleer.'

'Thank you, Madam,' said the cock, 'for your advice. But you are wrong. Listen to this story.'

Then Chantecleer told a story to prove that dreams come true.

---

1. **tips** : ends, e.g. fingertips.
2. **coward** : somebody who is always afraid.
3. **chemist** : a person who prepares and sells medicines.
4. **worms** : small creatures that live in the earth.
5. **swallow** : eat quickly without biting, e.g. to swallow medicine.

'Once,' he began, 'there were two men who visited another town on a pilgrimage. There was a great crowd of pilgrims and it was difficult to find a place to stay in the town. So they decided to sleep in separate inns. During the night, one of the men had a dream. His friend was calling out to him. "Please help me! Thieves have murdered me. Look at the blood on my clothes and face. They have stolen my money and hidden my body in a dung cart. [1] Tomorrow morning, come to the west gate of the city. You will find me there."'

Chantecleer paused. 'It was a horrible dream, full of blood and terror, but the man went back to sleep until the morning. When he woke up, he went to meet his friend at the other inn. But the innkeeper told him that his friend had gone. Quickly, he ran to the west gate of the city. He saw a dung cart leaving the town. So he called the sheriff [2] and asked him to search the cart.

'Is it necessary to tell you the end of the story, dear Pertelot? They found the murdered man in the cart. Murder will always come into the open.

'There are many other stories about dreams, my dear wife. They must be true. You can read them in the best books, even the Bible! So don't call me a coward.

'And now, Madam, the sun is rising. Come to me and let us enjoy ourselves together. It is time for love.'

With these words, Chantecleer forgot the dream and flew down into the yard and all his hens flew after him.

'Look at the great sun in the sky!' Chantecleer crowed. 'Cock-a-doodle-doo! It is the beginning of spring, my seven wives.

---

1. **dung cart** : a wagon for transporting all the dirt from the farm.
2. **sheriff** : the person responsible for the law in the town.

# The Nun's Priest's Tale

Oh Madam Pertelot, your beauty fills my heart. When I see how beautiful you are, I am not afraid. Cock-a-doodle-doo!'

But happiness always ends in sadness. There was a sly [1] fox with black tips on his ears and tail in the yard, under the vegetables, hiding like a murderer. He lay there until the middle of the day, waiting for the right time to run out and catch Chantecleer, the fat cock. He fixed his bright eyes on the delicious-looking [2] bird.

The cock followed his wife's advice. He ate some worms and walked proudly about the yard. Women are the reason for all the bad luck in the world. At least, that's what certain writers say. Not me. I don't believe it myself. Do you?

Pertelot and her sisters were lying in the warm sunlight. They washed their feathers and talked softly about love and food. Chantecleer walked freely and happily in the widow's farmyard, picking up worms and pieces of corn. Then suddenly, he saw the fox. It was the first time he had ever seen a fox but he was immediately afraid.

'Sir,' said the fox, 'why are you running away? I am your great friend and admirer. I came here especially to hear you sing. I knew your father and mother. They also had wonderful voices. They gave me great pleasure, especially when they came to my home.'

Chantecleer was very happy and proud. The stranger liked his singing!

The stupid bird stood on his toes. [3] He pushed up his neck

---

1. **sly** : clever in a secret, often cunning and deceitful way.
2. **delicious-looking** : seeming good to eat.
3. **toes** : 'fingers' are on the hands, 'toes' are on the feet.

towards the sky, puffed up [1] his chest, closed his eyes and opened his black, shining beak. He began to sing. But not for long!

It was all over [2] in a second!

The fox jumped. He caught Chantecleer by the neck, threw him over his back, and ran off towards the forest.

It was a terrible thing! Why had Chantecleer flown down into the yard? Why hadn't he stayed on the roof where he was safe? Why had his wife not believed in dreams? This great bird, the husband of seven wives, the handsomest creature in the world, the beautiful singer of morning love songs, is going to die! Greece lost its power. Rome burned. And Chantecleer, the cockerel, was stolen by a fox!

Pertelot and the hens screamed loudly. The widow ran out of her house and saw the fox. He was running towards the trees with Chantecleer over his shoulder. It was too late to stop him.

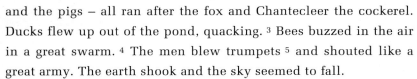

The widow, her two daughters, her servants with sticks, four dogs, the cook, the maid, even the cows, the sheep and the pigs — all ran after the fox and Chantecleer the cockerel. Ducks flew up out of the pond, quacking. [3] Bees buzzed in the air in a great swarm. [4] The men blew trumpets [5] and shouted like a great army. The earth shook and the sky seemed to fall.

---

1. **puffed up** : filled with air, made larger.
2. **it was all over** : it was finished.
3. **quacking** : making harsh sound.
4. **swarm** : a group of bees.
5. **trumpets** : brass musical instruments with a bright ringing tone.

**BLACK CAT ENGLISH CLUB**
The Commercial Press (Hong Kong) Ltd.
9/F, Eastern Central Plaza,
3 Yiu Hing Road, Shau Kei Wan,
Hong Kong

# BLACK CAT ENGLISH CLUB
## Membership Application Form

**BLACK CAT ENGLISH CLUB** is for those who love English reading and seek for better English to share and learn with fun together.

**Benefits offered:**
- Member Card
- Member badge, poster, bookmark
- Book discount coupon
- Black Cat English Reward Scheme
- English learning e-forum
- Surprise gift and more...

Simply fill out the application form below and fax it back to 2565 1113.

**Join Now! It's FREE** exclusively for readers who have purchased *Black Cat English Readers* !

The book(or book set) that you have purchased: _____

English Name: _____ (Surname) _____ (Given Name)

Chinese Name: _____

Address: _____

Tel: _____ Fax: _____

Email: _____

Sex: ❏ Male  ❏ Female                    (Login password for e-forum will be sent to this email address.)

Education Background: ❏ Primary 1-3      ❏ Primary 4-6    ❏ Junior Secondary Education (F1-3)
                     ❏ Senior Secondary Education (F4-5)   ❏ Matriculation
                     ❏ College           ❏ University or above

Age: ❏ 6 - 9        ❏ 10 - 12      ❏ 13 - 15      ❏ 16 - 18      ❏ 19 - 24      ❏ 25 - 34
                    ❏ 35 - 44      ❏ 45 - 54      ❏ 55 or above

Occupation:  ❏ Student      ❏ Teacher      ❏ White Collar      ❏ Blue Collar
             ❏ Professional   ❏ Manager      ❏ Business Owner    ❏ Housewife
             ❏ Others (please specify: _____ )

As a member, what would you like **BLACK CAT ENGLISH CLUB** to offer:

    ❏ Member gathering/ party    ❏ English class with native teacher    ❏ English competition
    ❏ Newsletter                 ❏ Online sharing                       ❏ Book fair
    ❏ Book discount              ❏ Others (please specify: _____ )

Other suggestions to **BLACK CAT ENGLISH CLUB:**

_____

Please sign here: _____

(Date: _____ )

g. Manna

Now, luck changed.

Chantecleer spoke to the fox as they arrived in the forest. The fox's teeth were sharply round his neck but he could just talk. 'You are safe now, sir. These stupid people who are running after us will never catch you. Turn round and shout at them. "You idiots, I am cleverer than all of you! Did you think you could catch Reynard the fox? You can't stop me now. I'll eat this cock for my supper." Then they will respect you, sir.'

The fox answered. 'Yes, you're right.' He opened his mouth and spoke. 'Idiots! I am cleverer than all of you. I'll eat this....'

But as soon as Reynard opened his mouth, Chantecleer got free. He flew high into the trees and sat on a branch looking down at the fox.

'Oh, Chantecleer,' called the fox, 'why have you flown away? Did I frighten you? I'm sorry, sir. Come down and I'll explain. I was not going to eat you — I simply wanted to bring you to my home so that you could sing for me and my children.'

'No,' said the cock, 'I won't be a fool twice. I'll never close my eyes and sing again when there's a fox in the yard!'

'And I'll never open my mouth to speak empty words,' said the fox.

'And that is the end of my tale,' said the Nun's Priest. 'It's only a story of a fox, a cock and a hen but we can all learn a lesson from it.'

'It was a good story,' agreed the Host. 'Don't you wish you had seven wives, like the cock? But you are a priest and can have none.'

# Comprehension and Opinion

**1** **How much did you understand?**

    **a.** What animals and birds did the widow have?

    **b.** What did Chantecleer dream about?

    **c.** What did Pertelot and Chantecleer disagree about?

    **d.** Why did the fox come to the farmyard?

    **e.** What happened when Chantecleer closed his eyes to sing?

    **f.** What happened when the fox opened his mouth to speak?

**2** **What do you think?**

Do dreams come true?

Does all the bad luck in the world come from women?

Does the story teach us anything?

# Animals and Birds

**3** **Here are the names of sixteen creatures.**

> **alligator    ant    beetle    cod    crocodile    dove**
> **housefly    goldfish    human being    lion    lizard**
> **pigeon    shark    sparrow    spider    whale**

**Divide them into five groups of three under these headings:**

| Birds | Fish | Insects | Mammals | Reptiles |
|-------|------|---------|---------|----------|
| ................. | ................. | ................. | ................. | ................. |
| ................. | ................. | ................. | ................. | ................. |
| ................. | ................. | ................. | ................. | ................. |
| ................. | ................. | ................. | ................. | ................. |
| ................. | ................. | ................. | ................. | ................. |

**Which creature belongs to none of these groups?**
**Can you add more names to each group? Use a dictionary if necessary.**

**Look at these names of parts of creatures:**

> antennae    beak    claws    comb    fangs    feathers
> fins    fur    scales    tail    whiskers    wings

**Write them in the correct places on the pictures.**

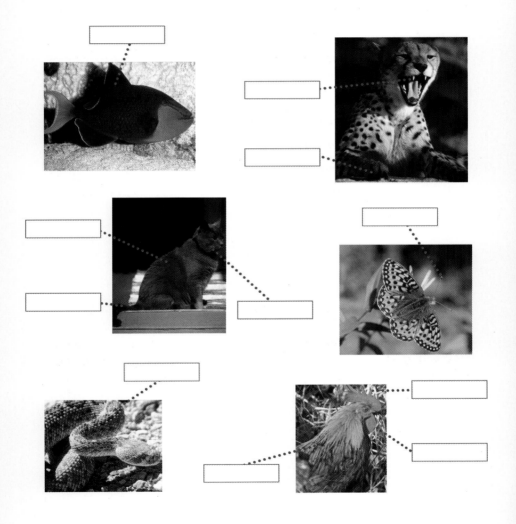

# The Dream of Drowning

FCE **4** You will hear another story about a dream: for questions 1-10 complete the sentences.

1.  Chantecleer told Pertolot some more ............................................. .

2.  Two merchants wanted to cross ................................................... .

3.  They waited in the port until the ................................................ .

4.  One of the travellers was worried because he had ........................

    ........................................................................................... .

5.  He wanted to ........................................................................ .

6.  His friend said that he wasn't afraid .......................................... .

7.  The friend decided to go to France and ...................................... .

8.  But during the journey there was ............................................... .

9.  The ship sank and every ........................................................... .

10. If Pertolot knew more history she wouldn't ...............................

    ........................................................................................... .


## Past Simple and Past Perfect

**When we are writing about the past, we can use the Past Perfect form of a verb to show that one action happened before another action. For example:**

FIRST: Palamon escaped from prison.

THEN: He went to the forest.

**After Palamon had escaped from prison, he went to the forest.**

**5** Here are some sentences about the story of the cock, the hen and the fox. In each sentence use one suitable verb in the Past Simple and one suitable verb in the Past Perfect. You can use verbs from this list. Some verbs can be used more than once.

> to be    to close    to come    to fly    to have    to love
>
> to open    to reach    to recover    to steal    to stop
>
> to seize    to tell    to thank    to walk    to want

**a.** But when Chantecleer ..................... his eyes to sing, the fox ..................... him.

**b.** After he ..................... from the shock of the dream, he ..................... around the farmyard.

**c.** The fox ..................... running when he ..................... the forest.

**d.** Pertelot ..................... Chantecleer since she ..................... a young chick.

**e.** One morning, Chantecleer ..................... his wife that he ..................... a terrible dream.

**f.** The cock ..................... up into the trees after the fox ..................... his mouth.

**g.** The fox ..................... Chantecleer that he ..................... to the farmyard to hear him sing.

**h.** After the priest ..................... his tale, the Host ..................... him.

**i.** Everyone ..................... to catch the fox who ..................... Chantecleer.

Put the sentences in the correct order by writing the letters (a-i) in the boxes:

☐ ☐ ☐ ☐ ☐ ☐ ☐ ☐ ☐

Now write a summary of the story. You can use some of these sentences but you need to add more.

# Writing – Strange Dreams

FCE 6 **For questions 1-26, read the text below and look carefully at each line. Some of the lines are correct, and some have a word which should not be there. If a line is correct, put a tick (✓) by the number below. If a line has a word which should not be there, write the word next to the number below. There are two examples at the beginning (0 and 00).**

## COMMON DREAMS AND THEIR MEANINGS

| | |
|---|---|
| There are many common dreams that most people have. | **0.** ✓ |
| Dreams that you are falling, that you are <u>not</u> naked in a | **00.** *not* |
| public place, or of losing your teeth are all dreams shared | **1.** ..... |
| out by a lot of people. To dream that you are taking an exam, | **2.** ..... |
| for example, indicates that you are being put to the test or | **3.** .... |
| being scrutinised in some way. Dreams in that your teeth are | **4.** ..... |
| falling out are one of the most of common dreams. | **5.** ..... |
| Such dreams are not only horrifying and shocking, but often | **6.** ..... |
| leave the dreamer with out a lasting image of the dream. One | **7.** ..... |
| theory about such dreams is that they reflect on your anxiety | **8.** ..... |
| about your appearance and how others see you. Another | **9.** ..... |
| explanation is they reflect your fear of being embarrassed or | **10.** ..... |
| making a fool of yourself in to some specific situation. | **11.** ..... |
| Flying dreams fall under a category of dreams where you | **12.** ..... |
| become aware of that you are dreaming, known as lucid | **13.** ..... |
| dreaming.  Many dreamers have described the ability to fly | **14.** ..... |
| in their dreams as an exhilarating, and joyful, and liberating | **15.** ..... |
| experience.  Flying with ease and looking down towards the | **16.** ..... |
| landscape below, suggests that you are not on top of a | **17.** ..... |
| situation or that you have risen above something. It may be | **18.** ..... |
| also mean that you have gained a different perspective on | **19.** ..... |
| things. If you are feeling fear when you are flying and or you | **20.** ..... |
| feel that you are flying too high, then as it suggests that you | **21.** ..... |
| are afraid of challenges and of success. It is quite fascinating | **22.** ..... |
| how ever people from different backgrounds and different | **23.** ..... |
| experiences can share these common themes. | **24.** ..... |
| The human mind has the ability to generate a myriad of | **25.** ..... |
| images, yet we can have to such similar dreams. | **26.** ..... |

⚜ PART FOUR ⚜

# The Pardoner's Tale

ne day, the Pardoner got drunk and told us all his secrets.

'I go into the churches and speak to the people.

*"You are all good people. But if anyone has stolen money from his neighbour or cheated* [1] *her husband with another man, they will go to Hell. But if you give me money, I will forgive you in the name of God."*

'Then they all hurry to give me gold. Who knows what happens after they die? – I don't care if they go to Heaven or Hell. I just want their money. Even the poor widow has something to give me. I have enough gold to buy a drink of wine and a girl in every town.

'But even a bad man like me can tell a good story. Listen to my tale.'

---

1.  **cheated** : been unfaithful to.

# The Pardoner's Tale

Some years ago, there was a group of young men who lived very badly. They danced and played music all day long. They loved eating and drinking, and afterwards they ran after the women of the town. Above all, they loved gambling. [1] They lived in a time of broken promises and lies and swearing. [2]

I am going to tell you about three of these bad young men. One Sunday they were sitting in a tavern, [3] drinking heavily instead of going to church. They heard a bell ringing. In the street, the people were taking a dead man to the churchyard. One of the men called the servant boy. 'Go and find out who has died. Make sure you get his name correctly.'

'I can tell you his name,' said the boy. 'He was one of your friends. But suddenly last night, he was killed. He was sitting at the table, completely drunk, when a silent thief named Death came and stabbed [4] him in the heart. Then the killer went away without a word. Death kills all of us round here. He has killed a thousand during the Plague. Be careful if you meet him, sirs. You see him everywhere you go. That's what my mother told me. It's all I know.'

The host of the tavern agreed. 'The boy's right. This year, Death killed everyone in a large village near here. Every man, woman and child was killed, the lords and the poor men. Death lives not far away. He's always appearing among us.'

---

1. **gambling** : playing cards etc. for money.
2. **swearing** : *(swear/swore/sworn)* using bad language.
3. **tavern** : inn or public house.
4. **stabbed** : killed with a knife.

'Great God, I'm not afraid!' said one of the young men. 'I'll look for this murderer, Death, in every street. I'll make a promise now. My brothers, let's drink together. We three are one! Death has killed our friends. Now, we will kill him before the day is finished!'

The three men stood up and drank. 'We will live and die for one another,' they promised. 'We are all brothers!' They went out of the tavern, completely drunk, and went towards the village where everyone had been killed. 'If we catch him, then Death is dead!'

On the way, they met a very old, very poor man. He was wrapped ¹ in old clothes so that they could hardly ² see his face. He greeted them politely. 'God be with you, my lords.'

'Get out of our way, you old fool,' said the leader of the men. 'Why do you live such a long time? It's time for an old man like you to die!'

'I have been all over the world, as far as India,' said the old man, 'but I cannot find a young man who will change his life for mine. So I live as an old man until God decides that I should die.

'Not even Death will take my life. So, like a prisoner in this world, I wait for my freedom. The earth is my mother. I knock on her gate with my stick and cry: Dear Mother! Let me in! Look at me! I am growing thinner every day. Wrap me in a sheet and take me into my grave! But she refuses to help me. So my face is white and my bones ache.'

The old man looked at the leader. 'You spoke very rudely to me just now. That is wrong. It says in the Bible that you should respect an old man with white hair. Don't hurt me, but treat me kindly so that, when you are old yourself, people will respect

---

1. **wrapped** : covered.  2. **hardly** : almost not.

you. Now let me pass. I must go where I must go.'

'No, old fool, you cannot escape from us so easily.' said the leader. 'You spoke about Death a few moments ago. Death has killed all our friends in this place. You are one of his spies! Tell us where he is or you'll pay for it. You are certainly one of Death's gang [1] who plan to kill all the young people. You wicked thief!'

'Well, sirs, if you really want to find Death, follow this crooked [2] path towards that forest. I left him there, under a tree. Can you see the oak? He's waiting for you there, I'm sure. He's not afraid of rude young men like you. Now God be with you and help you to become good.'

The three men ran down the crooked path towards the tree while the old man stood and watched. Then he continued on his journey.

What did they find under the tree? A huge pile of new gold coins!

They had never seen so much gold. They immediately forgot all about Death when they saw the shining money. It made them very happy.

The leader spoke first. 'Brothers, listen to me carefully. I have a plan. Luck has given us this treasure so that we can live happily and luxuriously [3] for the rest of our lives. We'll spend it all on pleasure. We didn't expect this to be our lucky day.

'We must take the gold away to my house as soon as possible. Or one of your houses. Brothers, we know that it is our gold. God has given it to us to make us happy. But we mustn't take it by day. People will think we are thieves. They will hang us because

---

1. **gang** : an organized group of criminals.
2. **crooked** : not straight.
3. **luxuriously** : in a very comfortable way.

# The Pardoner's Tale

of our treasure. We must take it away secretly at night. Therefore, one of us must go to the town to get bread and wine for us all while the others stay and look after the treasure. He must go quickly and secretly. Then, when it is dark, we will carry the gold to one of our houses. What do you think?'

They all agreed. They drew lots [1] and the youngest ran off to the town to get bread and wine. The other two stayed under the tree with the gold.

As soon as the youngest one had gone, the leader talked to the other. 'You are my true brother. We can help each other. You know that our companion has gone to the town. And here's a huge pile of gold which we will divide among the three of us. But if we divided it between two, that would be better for both of us. Do you agree, friend?'

'That's impossible,' said the other. 'He knows that we have the gold. If we take it all, how can we explain it to him?'

'Do you agree or not?' asked the first one. 'I can tell you my plan in a few words if you are interested.'

'Tell me. I will support you.'

'Well, we are two and he is only one. We are stronger than him. When he comes back, begin to wrestle [2] with him – he will think it is a game. Then I will come up secretly behind him and stab him in the back while you are fighting. Do the same. Stick your knife in his chest. Then, my dear friend, we will divide all this gold between the two of us, like brothers.'

So these two criminals decided to kill the third one as soon as he returned.

---

1. **drew lots** : (draw/drew/drawn) decided by chance.
2. **wrestle** : fight as a sport or a game.

But the youngest was also thinking about the gold as he ran to town. The shining coins were beautiful and bright. 'Oh God,' he thought, 'I would like all this gold for myself. No one would be as happy as I would be then.'

The Devil [1] put an idea in his head. 'I will poison my two companions,' he thought. He did not feel sorry for his friends. He only thought about the gold.

Immediately, he went to a chemist in the town. 'I need some poison to kill rats,' he said. 'Also, there's an animal which is killing my chickens at home. I must poison it.'

The chemist replied, 'I'll give you the strongest poison that I have. There is nobody, man or animal, that can take this poison and live. The smallest bit is enough to kill a man in a few minutes.'

The young man took the box of poison and left. He went to a shop in the next street and bought three bottles. He put the poison in two of the bottles but not in the third. He would drink from that bottle and enjoy the gold after his companions were dead. Then he filled the bottles with wine and went back to the tree.

I am near the end of my story. As they had agreed, the two other men killed the youngest one as soon as he returned with the wine. Then they sat down. 'Now let's sit and drink before we bury his body.'

The leader took one of the bottles, drank, and passed it to his friend who also drank. It was the poisoned wine. In a few minutes, all three were on the ground under the tree, ready for the rats and worms to eat them. They had found Death!

---

1. **the Devil** : the opposite of God, a bad power.

# Comprehension and Opinion

**1** **What happened in The Pardoner's Tale?**

    **a.** Why was the bell ringing in the street?

    **b.** What did the men decide to do?

    **c.** Where did the old man say they could find Death?

    **d.** How did they treat the old man?

    **e.** What did they find under the tree?

    **f.** Why did the youngest man go to the town?

    **g.** How did the three men die?

    **h.** Where did the old man say they could find Death?

    **i.** Who do you think the old man was?

    **j.** Do you think the men deserved to die?

    **k.** Do you think there are men like these in our society today?

## The First and Second Conditional

**When the leader of the men first had the idea of murder, he thought:**
A:  If we *killed* him, we *would have* more money for ourselves.

**Later, when the plan was more fixed, he thought:**
B:  If we *kill* him, we *will have* more money for ourselves.

**Look at A:**

| If | + | PAST SIMPLE VERB | CONDITIONAL VERB |
|----|---|------------------|------------------|
|    |   | *killed*         | *would have*     |

**This is a second conditional sentence. The murder is just a dream. We use the second conditional, when we are imagining something which is not real or not possible in the present. For example:**
*If I won a million pounds, I would buy a palace.*

**Look at B:**

| If | + | PRESENT SIMPLE VERB | FUTURE VERB |
|----|---|---------------------|-------------|
|    |   | *kill*              | *will have* |

**This is a first conditional sentence. The plan to kill him is real. The murder is possible!**

**2** **Now study these situations and, for each one, write a first or a second conditional sentence.**

a.  Tom has no car. His dream is to drive from England to China.
    Tom thinks: 'If I ............................................................................

b.  Tom has asked Susan to marry him. She will probably say 'yes'.
    They both want a lot of children.
    Tom thinks: ................................................................................

c.  Pete has just met Jane. He doesn't know her very well. But he
    dreams about marrying her and travelling round the world with her.
    Pete thinks: ...............................................................................

d.  Cambridge United are playing an important football match soon.
    Dan has bet a thousand pounds that they win. Cambridge have
    lost their last six matches.
    Dan thinks: .................................................................................

e.  Anne wants to work as a doctor in Africa. She is studying very hard
    for her final medical examinations next year. She is very intelligent.
    Anne thinks: ...............................................................................

f.  Gerry and Olivia want to rob the bank. They need money to go to
    the United States. But the bank is very well protected.
    They think: .................................................................................

g.  Gerry and Olivia find another bank. There are no guards. It is
    easy to break in.
    They think: .................................................................................

h.  The bank clerk, Mr Jones, is a coward. Gerry and Olivia ask him
    to give them the key to the safe. They are carrying guns.
    Mr Jones thinks: .........................................................................

i.  Gerry and Olivia are very confident. 'We are the best bank robbers
    in the world!' The police want to catch them and send them to
    prison for twenty years.
    Gerry and Olivia think: 'If the police ........................................

j.  Miss Timms hates criminals. She is near the alarm in the bank.
    She is not afraid of Gerry and Olivia.
    She thinks: .................................................................................

**3** Here are clues to fourteen words. All the words are connected with
death! Complete the words. Each dash represents a letter.

a. A box for a dead body       C _ _ _ _ _

b. The three men were...      M _ _ _ _ _ _ _ _

c. Another word for 'b'      K _ _ _ _ _ _

d. A place for dead people    C _ _ _ _ _ _ _

e. Another name for 'd'    G _ _ _ _ _ _ _

f. This person arranges 'j'    U _ _ _ _ _ _ _ _ _

g. 'k' is made up of these    B _ _ _ _

h. A place for 'b' after they die    H _ _ _

i. This symbolises pirates or poison    S _ _ _ _

j. A religious service for a dead person    F _ _ _ _ _ _

k. The hardest part of our bodies    S _ _ _ _ _ _ _

l. 'b' don't go here after they die    P _ _ _ _ _ _ _

m. The colour of death    B _ _ _ _

n. Dogs do this with 'g'    B _ _ _

Now read vertically straight down from the letter C in the first
word. The letters spell a well-known saying in English.

C _ _ _ _   _ _ _ S _ ' _   P _ _

# The Merchant's Tale

**4** Listen to the Merchant's Tale. For questions 1-9, tick (✓) the best
answers (A, B or C).

1. The Knight was called
   A ☐   February.
   B ☐   January.
   C ☐   July.

**2.** May was

**A** ☐ young and beautiful.

**B** ☐ young and rich.

**C** ☐ rich and old.

**3.** May was in love with

**A** ☐ January.

**B** ☐ Damian.

**C** ☐ her servant.

**4.** January became more jealous of May because

**A** ☐ he was blind.

**B** ☐ he held her hand.

**C** ☐ he knew she loved Damian.

**5.** May managed to be with Damian by

**A** ☐ leaving her husband in the garden.

**B** ☐ climbing into a pear tree.

**C** ☐ kissing her husband passionately.

**6.** Who gave January his sight back?

**A** ☐ May.

**B** ☐ Damian.

**C** ☐ The gods.

**7.** January saw May

**A** ☐ fighting Damian in the tree.

**B** ☐ kissing Damian in the tree.

**C** ☐ talking to the doctor.

**8.** May told January that

**A** ☐ he made a mistake.

**B** ☐ she loved Damian.

**C** ☐ she was kissing a young man.

**9.** What happened to Damian?

**A** ☐ He fell out of the tree.

**B** ☐ He escaped.

**C** ☐ He had pears for supper.

# A Good Story

**5** **Many people think that The Pardoner's Tale is the best story in *The Canterbury Tales*. Do you agree?**

Good stories usually have four important parts:

**PLOT**

The plot is the plan of the story. If the end of the story surprises us or if the story is cleverly planned, we usually enjoy the story more.

**CHARACTERS**

If the characters are well described or have recognisable personalities, it makes the story more interesting.

**THEMES**

The themes are the ideas of the story. One of the themes of the Pardoner's Tale is death, another is human selfishness and greed.

**STYLE**

Style is the way that the writer uses language and images to tell the story.

**Think about the films or plays you have seen and the books you have read. What is one of the best stories you know? Write a summary of the story by answering these questions:**

**a.** Where and when did it take place?

**b.** Who were the most important characters?

**c.** How did it begin?

**d.** What were the most important things which happened?

**e.** How did it end?

**f.** Why did you enjoy it?

# The City of Canterbury

Canterbury is the city of Becket's murder and of Chaucer's pilgrims. But it has a far longer history. There was an Iron Age settlement on the River Stour, Canterbury's small but important river, and Julius Caesar fought a battle against the Britons near Canterbury. The Romans built a walled city and named it Durovernum Cantiacorum.

Perhaps the most important event in Canterbury's history took place in 597 AD. Saint Augustine arrived from Rome. He met King Ethelbert, the most powerful ruler in England, and his Christian wife, Queen Bertha. As a result, Ethelbert and his people became Christians. Saint Augustine's Abbey was established and a cathedral was built. Canterbury became the religious centre of England.

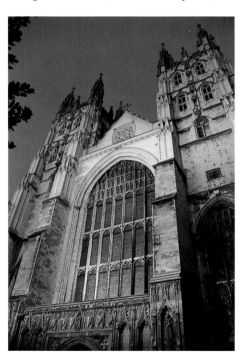

The Cathedral is of course the most important building in the city. It has developed over many centuries with different

*Henry II* (1133-1189) from Matthew Paris's Chronicles.

architectural [1] styles from Norman (Romanesque) to Victorian (19th century). The main part of the cathedral, however, is Gothic with a fine central tower called Bell Harry. Canterbury lies in a valley [2] so that when the pilgrims came down the hills towards it, they must have seen the cathedral dominating [3] the view.

A view of the Bell Harry tower.

There are many buildings which date from the time of the pilgrims. You can see the Eastbridge Hospital and the Poor Priests Hospital where pilgrims could rest. There are two important monasteries [4] on the river. Blackfriars was the home of the Dominicans who wore black and

A XVth century building nowadays used as a public house.

1. **architectural** : connected with the design of the building.
2. **valley** : a low place where a river flows between hills.
3. **dominating** : controlling.
4. **monasteries** : buildings in which monks live as a community.

Greyfriars was the home of the first Franciscans to come to England. An area just outside the city walls is called Wincheap which means 'wine market'. Pilgrims could buy wine there before they entered the religious heart of Canterbury where alcohol was not sold. But today there are as many pubs as churches in the city centre.

The Old Weavers' House and the river Stour.

The city has many other sights. King's School, just behind the cathedral, is the oldest 'public school' [1] in Britain. The medieval city walls have been re-built and one of the city gates, the Westgate with its two strong towers, remains. Saint Martin's church has the longest history of any church in England. The sixteenth century 'Weavers' House' is a fine wooden building near the river. However, Canterbury was badly bombed during the Second World War.

The Cathedral was undamaged but a large part of the historic city was lost.

You can still easily imagine Chaucer's pilgrims in Canterbury. The Pardoner and the Summoner hurried away to look for victims who would give them money. The Host and the Miller drank together in Wincheap. The Knight went to thank God for his victories in the

---

1. **public school** : in Britain, public schools are private.

Cathedral while his son, the Squire, walked along the bank of the River Stour with his chosen girl. The Merchant went to do business in Mercery Lane and the Wife of Bath searched for her sixth husband among the many pilgrims in the crowded city. They had arrived!

View of Christchurch Gate, the main entrance to the cathedral precincts, [1] seen from Mercery Lane.

**1** **Are these sentences true (T) or false (F)? Correct the false ones.**

|  | T | F |
|---|---|---|
| **a.** There was an Iron Age cathedral at Canterbury. | ☐ | ☐ |
| .................................................................................. | | |
| **b.** Saint Augustine succeeded in making the King a Christian. | ☐ | ☐ |
| .................................................................................. | | |

---

1. **precincts** : areas near or around a building.

**c.** The Cathedral is mainly Norman and Victorian in style.

□ □

...................................................................................................

**d.** Canterbury is on a hill so that it can be seen from far away.

□ □

...................................................................................................

**e.** The buildings from Chaucer's time were destroyed by bombs.

□ □

...................................................................................................

**f.** There are walls around the city.

□ □

...................................................................................................

**g.** There are two strong city gates which still stand.

□ □

...................................................................................................

**h.** The Wife of Bath got married in Canterbury.

□ □

...................................................................................................

T: GRADE 7

**2** **Topic - Village and city life**
**Choose a picture or an article about your favourite village or city in your country. Use it to talk about:**

1. Why you chose it. Why it is your favourite village or city.

2. Its origins. The origins of this place.

3. The advantages and disadvantages of the place. What you would like/dislike about living in this place.

4. How it compares with other villages/cities in your country. How life in this village or city compares with life in the place you live now.

PART FIVE

# The Wife of Bath's Tale

long time ago, when King Arthur ruled the land, there was a great knight who loved all the pleasures of life. But one day, a lady of the court told the King that the knight had attacked her.

Arthur was very angry and said that the knight must die. 'Cut off his head!' But the Queen and her ladies asked Arthur to give the knight to them for punishment. To please his queen, Arthur agreed.

The Queen sent for the knight. 'I and my ladies have the power to let you live or die,' she said. 'You will live only if you can answer this question: What is it that women most desire? If you cannot tell us at this moment, you may go away for a year and a

# The Wife of Bath's Tale

day to find the answer. But if you return without the answer, remember this: the axe is sharp!'

The knight was very unhappy but he had no choice. He said goodbye to the Queen and rode away.

He travelled through the whole country, from coast to coast, looking for the answer. He knocked on every door. 'What is it that women most desire?' he asked. But he could not find two people who agreed.

'Women want to be rich.'

'No, they want a good reputation.'

'No, they want pleasure.'

'They want fine clothes.'

'They want a life of love with many husbands.'

'Women want to be spoilt and flattered.' [1]

'Women want freedom, with nobody to criticise them.'

'Women want people to say that they can keep a secret.'

That is nonsense, of course. No woman can keep a secret. Do you remember the ancient tale of King Midas? Midas grew a splendid pair of donkey's ears under his long hair. Nobody knew except his wife. Midas loved her and made her promise that she wouldn't tell anyone about his ears. Of course, she promised but, because she was a woman, it was difficult to keep the secret. It wanted to fly out of her mouth.

'I must tell somebody,' she thought. So, she ran down to the lake, her heart on fire. She lay down among the river grasses and whispered the secret to the water. 'My husband has a pair of

---

1. **flattered** : told nice things about themselves.

donkey's ears.' The wind spread the secret through the whole country. We women are all like that.

Well, the knight realised that he would never find the answer. He felt sad and hopeless. The year had finished and this was the day when he had to return to the Queen.

As he was riding sadly back to the court through the forest, he suddenly saw twenty-four beautiful women dancing on the green grass. 'Perhaps they know the answer,' he thought. He approached them but, as he did so, they vanished [1] from his sight. It had been a magic vision. Remember that, in the days of King Arthur, there were still fairies in the world.

There was no living thing in the forest except an old woman sitting on the grass where they had danced. She was the ugliest, most horrible creature he had ever seen.

This ugly hag [2] stood up and said, 'Sir knight, there is no path here. Tell me, what are you looking for? Perhaps I can help. We old people know many things.'

'Old lady, I will die today unless I can answer this question. What is it that women most desire? If you can tell me, I'll pay you well.'

'Give me your hand,' said the hag. 'Promise me that, if I give you the true answer, you will do anything that I ask.'

'I promise,' agreed the knight.

'Then your life is safe. The Queen herself will agree with my answer. The proudest lady that ever wore beautiful clothes will admit that I am right. Let me teach you the answer.' And the old woman whispered in his ear.

---

1. **vanished** : disappeared suddenly and completely.
2. **hag** : ugly old woman.

When they came to the Queen's court, the knight said, 'I am ready to give my answer.'

The Queen and all her ladies were there. There were single women and wives and many widows, who are the wisest of all. The knight was the only man, surrounded [1] by women. 'Speak!' said the Queen who sat like a judge. 'Silence everyone. Listen to the knight.'

The knight spoke loudly so that all the ladies could hear. 'My sweet Queen,' he said, 'women desire to have power over their husbands. This is your greatest desire. Kill me if you like but this is the true answer.'

There was no woman in the court, not a girl or a wife or a widow, who disagreed with him. 'You may keep your life!' said the Queen.

At that moment, the old hag jumped up and spoke. 'Oh powerful Queen,' she said, 'before you go, give me justice. I taught the knight how to answer. In return, he said that he would do whatever I asked him. Therefore, before this court, I ask you, sir knight, to marry me. I have saved your life; now do this for me.'

The knight answered unhappily. 'I know that I promised you this. But please change your request. I will give you everything I have but let my body be mine.'

'No! I am ugly and old and poor. But I do not want gold or land or luxuries. I want to be your wife and, more than that, I want to be your love!'

'My love? That is impossible.'

But the knight could not escape. He married the hag secretly

---

1. **surrounded** : encircled.

next day and hid himself for the rest of the day. There was no dancing, no singing or eating and drinking at their wedding.

That night, he lay in bed with her. He turned to and fro [1] like someone with a bad dream, keeping as far away from her as possible.

His old wife lay there smiling. 'Dear husband, does every one of King Arthur's knights behave like this with his bride? I am your own sweet wife. I have saved your life. I have never done anything bad to you. Why do you behave like this on our first night together? Tell me the problem and I will make it right.'

'Make it right? No, impossible. You are so ugly, so old, and you come from such a low family, that I don't want to be near you.'

'Is that all? If you treat me well, I can make this right in three short days. But why do you worry about my family? Don't you know that true gentlewomen and true gentlemen are the ones who do good things. Lords and ladies can become thieves and murderers and cheats. [2] But a poor man or woman can be a true gentle-person if he or she loves God and other human beings.

'Then you say that I am poor. There is nothing wrong in that. Jesus himself chose to live as a poor man. I think that the poor man is rich, even if he has no shirt. The poor man can always find a song to sing. He is not afraid of thieves. He loves God. He knows that his friends love him for himself and not for his money. It is good to be poor, I think.

'Lastly, you said that I am old and ugly. But you know that all the best writers tell us to respect old people. And if I'm ugly, you needn't be afraid that I will cheat you with another man. But I know what men like. I will give you great pleasure.

---

1. **turned to and fro** : turned from side to side continuously.
2. **cheats** : people who act dishonestly in order to win profit.

# The Wife of Bath's Tale

'Now, choose one of these two things. You can have me old and ugly until I die. I will be a true wife to you and never upset you as long as I live. Or you can have me young and beautiful. But then men will visit your house while you are away because I am so beautiful. Now choose. Which do you want?'

The knight thought about this for a long time. It made him very unhappy. At last, he spoke.

'My lady and my love, my darling wife, I put myself in your power. Choose yourself. You are wise enough to know which way is the best for you and for me. I don't care what you decide. If you are pleased, then I am also happy.'

'Are you really giving me the power to choose? Will you do as I say?'

'Yes, wife, it is best.'

'Then kiss me. We'll stop being angry with each other. I'll be both things to you. I mean that I'll be young and beautiful but also a true wife. I'll be the best wife that anyone has ever had in the history of the world. If, tomorrow, when the sun is shining, I am not as beautiful as any queen in the east or west, then kill me if you like. Take the curtain from the window. It is morning already, husband. Look at me.'

When the knight looked at her, he saw that she really was young and beautiful. He caught her in his arms and gave her a thousand kisses. She did everything she could to please him.

So they lived in perfect joy. Please God, send all of us women young, strong, handsome husbands who will do anything for our love. And if any men won't give women what they most desire – the power over their husbands – let God strike them dead!

# Comprehension and Opinion

**1** **Do you understand The Wife of Bath's Tale?**

    **a.** What was the Queen's question?

    **b.** What did the knight see in the forest?

    **c.** What did he promise to the hag?

    **d.** What did she ask him to do?

    **e.** Give three reasons why the knight didn't love his wife.

    **f.** Why was the hag pleased by the knight's choice?

**2** **What do you think?**

Was the answer to the question correct?

What do modern women want?

Do men and women want the same things?

**3** **What do men and women want? Here is a list of adjectives. Change them into nouns. The first one has been done for you.**

affectionate: affection    beautiful: ..................    comfortable: ...........

famous: ....................    free: ..........................    happy: ....................

healthy: ..................    independent: ...........    luxurious: .............

respectful: ..............    successful:.................    wealthy: .................

**Now write sentences about what people want, using either adjectives or nouns.**

Begin: 'Women/Men/People/Most people/Some people want.....

For example: People want their partners to be affectionate.

      or People want affection from others.

**Write other sentences using your own ideas.**

# Another Proverb

**4** **Here is another English proverb. Each number represents a letter.**

1.2.3.3.4.    5.6.    7.2.8.9.10.,    3.10.11.10.6.9.    2.9.
12.10.5.8.13.3.10.

**If you can find the words below, you will be able to understand the proverb:**

**a.** Between men and women, there is
the battle of the:                          8. 10. **X** 10. 8.

**b.** Someone who defends the rights of
women is a:                             **F** 10. 1. 5 .6. 5. 8. 9.

**c.** A strong disagreement is a:        **Q** 13. 2. 3. 3. 10. 12.

**d.** A ..... wife or husband always complains:    6. 2. **G G** 5. 6. **G**

**e.** The more powerful person in a marriage
wears the:                            9. 3. **O** 13. 8. 10. 3. 8.

**f.** To talk about other people's business is
to ..... . Do men or women do this more?    **G O** 8. 8. 5. 11.

**g.** Somebody who plays with love is a:    **F** 12. 5. 3. 9.

**h.** Telling your friend that he/she is the most
handsome/beautiful person in the world is:    **F** 12. 2. 9. 9. 10. 3. 4.

**i.** Another proverb says that the way to a
man's heart is through his:               8. 9. **O** 1. 2. **C** 7.

**j.** In other words, men prefer food to:    **B** 10. 2. 13. 9. 4.

**Now write the proverb here. You may need a dictionary to help you understand it.**

_ _ _ _ _   _ _   _ _ _ _ _,   _ _ _ _ _ _   _ _   _ _ _ _ _ _ _

# The Wife of Bath

**FCE** **5** **Listen to the Wife of Bath talking about her life. For questions 1-10, tick (✓) the correct answers true (T) or false (F).**

|  | | T | F |
|---|---|---|---|
| 1. | The Wife of Bath was twelve years old when she was first married. | ☐ | ☐ |
| 2. | She has had six husbands. | ☐ | ☐ |
| 3. | Her first three husbands controlled her. | ☐ | ☐ |
| 4. | She became rich because of them. | ☐ | ☐ |
| 5. | She thinks that money is more important than love. | ☐ | ☐ |
| 6. | Her fourth husband was more difficult to control. | ☐ | ☐ |
| 7. | She treated him badly. | ☐ | ☐ |
| 8. | She gave him an expensive funeral. | ☐ | ☐ |
| 9. | She is no longer interested in love. | ☐ | ☐ |
| 10. | She has been a good wife to all her husbands. | ☐ | ☐ |

**6** **The Wife of Bath has strong beliefs about life. Listen again and supply the missing words in a-e.**

a. Real ............................. comes from experience.

b. Everything is for ........................... .

c. Why spend money ............. ...................... ...........................?

d. I've had a ............................. of love.

e. Although I've lost my ........................ ....................................,
   I still know how to .................. ...................... ...................... .

## Asking Questions

**Look at these questions:**

TYPE ONE:     ***What did*** the knight do?
              ***What do*** women most desire?

TYPE TWO:     ***Who*** helped the knight?
              ***How many*** ladies danced in the forest?

**Type One questions use 'do' or 'did' to form the question. The answer is *not* the *subject* of the verb:**

He *attacked a lady.*          They desire *power.*

**Type Two questions don't use 'do' or 'did'. The answer is the *subject* of the verb.**

*The hag* helped the knight.     *24 ladies* danced there.

**7** **Now make questions about *The Tales*.**

    **a.** The fox hid under the vegetables.
    Who .............................................? The fox.
    Where .........................................? Under the vegetables.

    **b.** Theseus put the cousins in the tower.
    Who .............................................? The cousins.
    Where .........................................? In the tower.
    Who .............................................? Theseus.

    **c.** The two men planned the murder.
    Why ...............................................? Because they wanted the gold.
    How many men ............................? Two.

    **d.** The Host suggested a competition.
    Who .............................................? The Host.
    What ...........................................? A competition.

    **e.** The knight married the hag the next day.
    Why ..............................................? Because she had helped him.
    Who .........................................? The hag.

# This is my Life

**8** **The Wife of Bath has the strongest character of all the pilgrims. Most readers of *The Canterbury Tales* remember her longest. Listen to her life story on the recording again.**

**What are the facts of her life:**

**a.** When did she first get married?

**b.** How many husbands has she had?

**c.** What happened to them? Has she travelled?

**Here are some facts about some modern characters.**

> **A soldier.** **Born:** 1915. **Married:** three times.
> 1: a film actress
> 2: an aristocrat
> 3: a fashion model
>
> Twelve children, eighteen grandchildren.
>
> Six medals in the Second World War.
>
> **OPINIONS:** The world was better in the past.
> A soldier's life is the best.

> **An opera singer. Born:** 1965.      Never married.
>
> **Performances:** Milan, New York, Paris, London, Tokyo etc.
>
> **Books:** 'My Life' volumes I, II, III and IV.
>
> **Her friends include:** presidents, kings, queens, princesses,
>   Nobel prize winners, Olympic champions etc.
>
> **OPINIONS:** Marriage is for fools.
> Life is wonderful.

**Choose one of these characters or imagine another character. Write a monologue;** [1] **he/she is telling his/her life story to an audience, like the Wife of Bath.**

---

1.   **monologue** : long speech in a play spoken by one actor/actress.

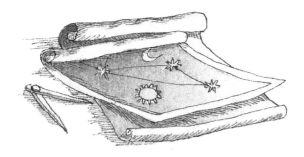

# The Franklin's Tale

'I am a simple man,' said the Franklin. 'I haven't read many books. But I will tell my story simply and clearly.'

A long time ago, in Brittany, there was a knight who loved a lady. She was one of the most beautiful women under the sun and came from a noble family. He was afraid to speak to her but at last he asked her to marry him.

She knew how much he loved her and decided to accept him as her husband and her lord. In return, he promised that he would never use his power against her but would always do what she wanted. He would never forget that he was her lover as well as her husband.

'Sir,' she said, 'you have given me everything I want from marriage – love and independence. I will be your true wife until I die. My heart is yours.'

# The Canterbury Tales

This is the best kind of marriage. Love will not be limited by power. When one person tries to control the other, the God of Love beats his wings and, farewell, he is gone! Women want to be free, not to be servants. And men are the same.

So the lady took the knight as her servant in love and her lord in marriage. If you are not married, you can't imagine the happiness that a wife and husband can enjoy.

Soon, however, the knight, whose name was Arveragus, had to go to England to fight. He stayed there for two years. His wife, whose name was Dorigen, loved her husband as much as she loved her own life. While he was away, she cried and sighed [1] and lost her appetite. She could not sleep and paid no attention to the world. Arveragus sent her letters, telling her how much he loved her. At last, she began to recover. [2] She drove away her dark fantasy.

Her castle was on the coast, next to the sea. Dorigen often walked with her friends along the cliff-top [3] but, when she saw the ships on the sea, she began to cry. 'If one of these ships brought home my lord, then my heart would be happy.'

There were terrible black rocks in the sea. Her heart trembled with fear. 'God, why did you make these black rocks and put them here in the sea? They are no good for anything. They destroy ships. Thousands of men have died at sea. It kills my heart to look at them.'

One morning in May, her friends had a party for her. They wanted to make her happy. They went to a garden full of flowers

---

1. **sighed** : breathed deeply and sadly.
2. **recover** : become well again.
3. **cliff-top** : a high hill above the sea.

with their bright colours and sweet perfumes; a little paradise. After dinner, they began to dance and sing. But Dorigen stayed alone. She could not be happy without Arveragus.

At this party, there was one of her neighbours, a young squire named Aurelius. He was as bright and handsome as May itself. He was young, strong, honest, rich and wise; a perfect lover. He had loved Dorigen secretly for two years but had never told her. He had written many songs and poems about a beautiful lady that he loved hopelessly but she herself had no idea that she was the lady!

Aurelius decided that the time had come to open his heart.

'Madam, my heart is breaking. You can kill me or save my life with one word. I lie here at your feet. Give me your sweet love or I will die.'

'What are you saying?' said Dorigen. 'I will never be an untrue wife. Take this as my final answer.' But, after this, she added as a joke, 'Aurelius, I would give you my love if you could remove the black rocks from the sea. If you can do that, I'll love you more than any other man!'

'Is there no other way to win your love?'

'No, by God. Forget this stupid idea. Why do you want another man's wife?'

'Madam,' said Aurelius, 'it is impossible to remove the rocks. So, I will die for your love.' With these words, he left her. At his house, he shivered [1] with cold. His heart was ice. He got down on his knees and spoke to the gods.

'Apollo, god of the sun, help me. Your sister, the goddess of the moon, has power over the seas and rivers. Ask her to make a

---

1. **shivered** : shook slightly.

# Comprehension and Opinion

**1** **What happened in The Franklin's Tale?**

    **a.** What do both men and women want in marriage?

    **b.** What did Dorigen see in the sea?

    **c.** Did Dorigen expect that Aurelius could remove the rocks?

    **d.** Why did Aurelius go to Orléans?

    **e.** What did Dorigen decide to do?

    **f.** Why didn't the magician want his payment?

**2** **What do you think?**

Do you believe in magic?

Did Arveragus do the right thing?

Did Dorigen and Arveragus have the perfect marriage?

# Phrasal Verbs

**3** **Here are some common phrasal verbs. Fill the gap in each example sentence by using the verb in the Past Simple tense.**

    **a.** *to break out:* A fight ..................... in the street last night.

    **b.** *to bring about:* The new manager ..................... a victory.

    **c.** *to fall out with:* The Wife of Bath ..................... her husbands.

    **d.** *to give up:* She ..................... smoking.

    **e.** *to look after:* Doctor Soames ..................... my sick brother.

    **f.** *to look for:* The police ..................... the robbers.

    **g.** *to put forward:* The committee member ..................... a suggestion.

    **h.** *to put off:* He ..................... the party until the summer.

    **i.** *to put on:* They ..................... dry clothes after the rainstorm.

    **j.** *to set off:* The travellers ..................... early from the port.

Now complete the sentences with the phrasal verbs provided in Exercise 3 (a-j) in suitable forms.

**a.** The Prioress ............................... her little dogs lovingly.

**b.** War ............................... between Athens and Thebes.

**c.** Aurelius ............................... everything in order to win Dorigen.

**d.** Palamon ............................... Arcite because of Emily.

**e.** The magician ............................... the disappearance of the rocks.

**f.** Aurelius wanted to ............................... paying the magician.

**g.** The pilgrims ............................... from the Tabard Inn.

**h.** The three men ............................... Death.

**i.** Arcite ............................... a disguise when he returned to Athens.

**j.** The Host ............................... the idea of a competition.


# The Book against Women

 **4** **Listen to The Franklin's Tale on the recording. You will hear the Wife of Bath telling the story of her fifth husband.**
**Listen once or twice and answer the questions.**

**a.** What was special about her last husband?

**b.** Was his name Jenkin or Jankin or Junkin?

**c.** Where did they first meet?

**d.** What did she say to him while they were walking?

**e.** How soon after the end of her fourth marriage did she marry again?

**f.** What was the book like?

**g.** What kind of stories were in the book?

**h.** How many pages did she tear out of [1] the book?

**i.** Why is the Wife of Bath deaf?

---

1. **tear out of** : *(tear/tore/torn)* remove violently.

**j.**  Why was he worried?

**k.**  What did he promise?

**l.**  What happened to the book?

**m.**  Do you think that she really loved him?


## The Past Simple and the Present Perfect Passive

**Look at these sentences:**

They murdered Thomas Becket in the cathedral.
(PAST SIMPLE ACTIVE)

People have remembered Thomas Becket until now.
(PRESENT PERFECT ACTIVE)

**'Thomas Becket' is the most important part of these sentences. We can emphasise this by using the passive. Now the sentences begin: 'Thomas Becket...'**

Thomas Becket was murdered in the cathedral.
(PAST SIMPLE PASSIVE: *was* or *were* + *the past participle*)

Thomas Becket has been remembered until now.
(PAST PERFECT PASSIVE: *has* or *have* + *been* + *the past participle*)

Remember that we use the Past Simple for an event in the past that is finished. We use the Present Perfect for an event that has happened in the time period between **then** and **now**. The Present Perfect is often used with **since, ever, never, recently**, etc.


**5** Now use the verbs below in the Past Simple or Present Perfect passive form to complete the sentences (a-j). Some words can be used more than once.

> **to bomb    to build    to bury    to destroy**
> **to discover    to read    to translate**
> **to visit    to write**

**a.**  Chaucer's stories ............................... for hundreds of years.

**b.**  *The Canterbury Tales* ............................... in the fourteenth century.

**c.** Canterbury ................................ by thousands of pilgrims until the shrine ................................ by Henry VIII.

**d.** Canterbury ................................ by pilgrims and tourists ever since Becket's death.

**e.** Chaucer ................................ in Westminster Abbey in 1400.

**f.** *The Canterbury Tales* ................................ into modern English many times since then.

**g.** The bones of Becket ........................... (never) ........................... .

**h.** ................................ Chaucer's work ever ................................ into Italian?

**i.** Canterbury ................................ during the  Second World War but the cathedral ................................ (not) ............................... .

**j.** Many new shops ................................ in Canterbury since the 1950's.

**6** It is very difficult to read Chaucer in the original, because he wrote in Middle English. This is very different from modern English. But here are a few famous lines as Chaucer wrote them. Can you understand them? There is a rough translation to help you. What are the missing words in the modern translation?

FROM THE PROLOGUE:

Whan that Aprille with his shoures sote
The droghte of March hath perced to the rote...
Than longen folk to go on pilgrimages.
(When .............. with its sweet showers replaces the dry period of .............., then people desire to go on .............. .)

FROM THE KNIGHT'S TALE:

She gadereth floures, party white and rede,
To make a sotyil garland for her hede,
And as an angel hevenly she songe.
(She gathered white and red .............. to decorate her head and sang like a heavenly .............. .)

**FROM THE NUN'S PRIEST'S TALE:**

Wommannes counseil brought us first to wo,
And made Adam from paradys to go...
(.............. advice brought the first unhappiness and made Adam
leave .............. .)

**FROM THE PARDONER'S TALE:**

Ther came a privee theef, men clepeth Deeth,
That in this contree al the peple sleeth,
And with his spear he smoot his herte a-two...
(A secret .............. came, called Death, who kills everyone in this
area, and broke his .............. in two with his spear.)

**FROM THE WIFE OF BATH'S TALE:**

And eek I preye Jesu short hir lyves
That wol nat be governed by hir wives...
(and also I .............. that God will shorten the lives of husbands who
will not be controlled by their .............. .)

**FROM THE FRANKLIN'S TALE:**

Love wol not ben constreyned by maistrye;
Whan maistrie cometh, the god of love anon
Beteth hise winges, and farewel! he is gon!
(Love will not be limited by power; when power enters a marriage,
the god of love soon beats his .............. and – goodbye! – he goes!)

A French illumination of Emily being watched by Palamon and Arcite.

# INTERNET PROJECT

Using a search engine find a site on the Internet which contains *The Canterbury Tales* in modern English.

Then choose another Tale which wasn't included in this collection, read it and write a short summary in English.

## Writing a story

**2** Go back and choose an illustration. For example, page 95 shows Dorigen looking out towards the sea with a castle on a cliff nearby. Either use the illustration to invent your own story or if you prefer describe the picture in detail. Remember to include information about:

1. the surroundings
2. the objects
3. the weather
4. the atmosphere
5. the time of day/year

If you are writing a story, remember to invent names for the characters you see.

.................................................................................................

.................................................................................................

.................................................................................................

.................................................................................................

.................................................................................................

# EXIT TEST

**1** The following questions are about all the stories. For questions 1-8, tick (✓) the answers (A, B, C or D) which you think fit best according to the text.

1. Chaucer met the pilgrims
   A ☐ in Canterbury.
   B ☐ at the tomb of Thomas Becket.
   C ☐ in London.
   D ☐ in the forest.

2. How many people were in the group when they left early in the morning?
   A ☐ 29.
   B ☐ 30.
   C ☐ 31.
   D ☐ 32.

3. Theseus decides to let Arcite and Palamon live because
   A ☐ they are no longer the enemies of Athens.
   B ☐ what they have done, they have done for love.
   C ☐ he is in love with Emily.
   D ☐ he wants to watch them fight.

4. Chantecleer's dream
   A ☐ is a result of eating too much.
   B ☐ comes true.
   C ☐ makes him laugh.
   D ☐ is about a coward.

5. The fox releases Chantecleer from his mouth because
   A ☐ Chantecleer tricks him.
   B ☐ Chantecleer is too heavy.
   C ☐ he wants Chantecleer to sing.
   D ☐ Chantecleer is stupid.

6. What do the three young men ultimately find under the tree?
   A ☐ A pile of gold.
   B ☐ The old man.
   C ☐ Death.
   D ☐ Poison.

7. The Knight tells his wife that he wants her
   A ☐ to be young and beautiful.
   B ☐ to be old, ugly and true.
   C ☐ to decide for herself.
   D ☐ to go away.

8. Dorigen promises Aurelius her love if
   A ☐ he removes the black rocks from the sea.
   B ☐ he writes her songs and poems.
   C ☐ he dies for her.
   D ☐ Arveragus returns home safely.

Score ⬭

## 2 Answer the following questions.

1. How many pilgrims were there on the pilgrimage?

2. According to Chaucer, who were the two bad people of the group and why were they bad?

3. In the Knight's Tale why do Arcite and Palamon fight? Who wins in the end?

4. How does Chantecleer manage to escape from the fox in the Nun's Priest's Tale?

5. If the three men in the Pardoner's Tale had been less selfish would they have found death? Why?/Why not?

6. In the Wife of Bath's Tale what is women's greatest desire?

7. Why does Aurelius release Dorigen from her obligation to him in the Franklin's tale?

Score ⬭

**3** The tales contain many different themes. Below is a list of the most important ones in the stories you have read. Match them to the correct tales. You can use a theme more than once.

generosity    greed    dreams    love    friendship    pride
misogyny [1]    bravery    chivalry    deception    role of fate
relationship between husband and wife    magic

The Knight's Tale ...........................................................................
The Nun's Priest's Tale ...................................................................
The Pardoner's Tale ........................................................................
The Wife of Bath's Tale ...................................................................
The Franklin's Tale .........................................................................

Score

# Writing

**4** Which tale do you enjoy the most? And which one do you like the least? Then write a short paragraph justifying your answers.

---

1.  **misogyny** : hatred for women.

# The Canterbury Tales

## KEY TO THE ACTIVITIES AND EXIT TEST

### THE LIFE OF GEOFFREY CHAUCER

**Page 12   Exercise 1**

**1.** C   **2.** A   **3.** A   **4.** A   **5.** B
**6.** B   **7.** C   **8.** C

### CHAUCER'S WORLD

**Page 16   Exercise 1**

**a.** Edward III, Richard II, Henry IV.
**b.** France.
**c.** The Plague, a terrible disease.
**d.** God is deaf.
**e.** The Pardoner, Summoner, Prioress.
**f.** In Canterbury Cathedral.
**g.** She was on a pilgrimage.
**h.** April.

### INTERNET PROJECT

**Suggested web sites:**

http://icg.fas.harvard.edu/~chaucer/special/varia/life_of_Ch/chrono.html

http://www.librarius.com/chauchro.htm

### SUMMARY

**Page 18   Exercise 1**

Open answers.

## PART ONE

### THE PROLOGUE

**Page 26   Exercise 1**

**a.** At the Tabard Inn at night.
**b.** Because he was young and handsome.
**c.** Yes, she loved her little dogs.
**d.** She was wearing a huge hat, a long coat, red tights and new shoes.
**e.** No, they only cared about money and power.
**f.** He wanted all the pilgrims to tell stories.

**Page 26   Exercise 2**

Open answers.

**Page 26   Exercise 3**

**Jewellery:** bracelet, brooch, ear-rings, necklace, pendant, ring.

**h.** had told/thanked

**i.** wanted/had stolen

Order: d e b g a i c f h

## Page 61   Exercise 6

**1.** of    **2.** out    **3.** ✓    **4.** in    **5.** of
**6.** ✓    **7.** out    **8.** on    **9.** ✓    **10.** ✓
**11.** to    **12.** ✓    **13.** of    **14.** ✓
**15.** and    **16.** ✓    **17.** not    **18.** be
**19.** ✓    **20.** and    **21.** as    **22.** ✓
**23.** ever    **24.** ✓    **25.** ✓    **26.** to

# PART FOUR

## THE PARDONER'S TALE

## Page 70   Exercise 1

**a.** Because the people were taking a dead body to the churchyard.

**b.** They decided to kill Death.

**c.** In the forest under a tree.

**d.** They were rude to him.

**e.** They found a huge pile of gold coins.

**f.** He went to the town to get some bread and wine.

**g.** The youngest one was murdered. The others were poisoned when they drank the wine.

**h.** Under a tree.

**i.** Death.

**j.** Open answer.

**k.** Open answer.

## Page 71   Exercise 2

**a.** If I had a car, I would drive from England to China.

**b.** If I marry Susan, we will have a lot of children.

**c.** If I married Jane, I would travel round the world with her.

**d.** If Cambridge United won, I would

win the bet.

**e.** If I pass my examinations, I will work in Africa.

**f.** If we robbed the bank, we would go to the United States.

**g.** If we rob the bank, we will go to the United States.

**h.** If I don't give them the money, they will shoot me.

**i.** If the police caught us, we would go to prison.

**j.** If I ring the bell, the police will catch them.

## Page 72   Exercise 3

**a.** coffin    **b.** murderers    **c.** killers
**d.** cemetery    **e.** graveyard
**f.** undertaker    **g.** bones    **h.** Hell
**i.** skull    **j.** funeral    **k.** skeleton
**l.** Paradise    **m.** black    **n.** bury
Crime doesn't pay.

## Page 72   Exercise 4

**1.** B    **2.** A    **3.** B    **4.** A    **5.** B
**6.** C    **7.** B    **8.** A    **9.** B

### Tapescript

*Once, there was a rich old knight who had a beautiful young wife. They were called January and May. January was very jealous of his wife and watched her very carefully. But January's servant, Damian, sent her secret love-letters. May wanted to meet Damian alone but it was difficult with such a jealous husband.*

*One day, January woke up and could not see. He was blind. He became more and more jealous because he couldn't watch his wife. All day and all night, he held May's hand. It was even more difficult than before to meet Damian.*

May, however, made a plan to trick her old, blind husband. She led him into the garden. Damian had climbed a tree and was sitting in the branches. 'Darling husband,' said May, 'help me to climb into the tree. There are some delicious pears. I will bring you one.' January agreed. May stood on his back and climbed into the tree above his head. At last she was free. May and Damian kissed passionately among the green leaves and the golden fruit. But the gods were watching. They decided to help January. They gave him back his sight. He could see again! And the first thing he saw was his young wife kissing his servant in the pear tree.

'Wife!' he shouted angrily. 'What are you doing?'

May thought quickly. 'A doctor told me,' she said, 'that the only way to help you to see again was to fight with a young man in a tree. It's magic! I did it to help you, darling.'

'But you weren't fighting, you were kissing,' said January.

'Your eyes are not so good yet. You made a mistake. Of course I wasn't kissing that young man,' she answered.

She came down from the tree and kissed him while Damian escaped. 'Everything is all right,' she said. 'You can see again, my darling husband, and we have some delicious pears for our supper.'

## Page 74   Exercise 5
Open answers.

## THE CITY OF CANTERBURY

### Page 78   Exercise 1
a. False – There was an Iron Age settlement.
b. True
c. False – The Cathedral has many different architectural styles.
d. False – Canterbury is in a valley.
e. False – There are still many buildings from Chaucer's time.
f. True
g. False – There is one city gate which still stands.
h. False – She looked for her sixth husband among the many pilgrims.

### Page 79   Exercise 2
Open answers.

# PART FIVE

## THE WIFE OF BATH'S TALE

### Page 88   Exercise 1
a. What is it that women most desire?
b. He saw twenty-four beautiful women dancing.
c. He promised to do anything that she asked.
d. She asked him to marry her.
e. She came from a low-class family. She was poor. She was old and ugly.
f. Because he gave her the power to choose.

### Page 88   Exercise 2
Open answers.

## Page 88   Exercise 3

beauty   comfort   fame   freedom
happiness   health   independence
luxury   respect   success   wealth

## Page 89   Exercise 4

**a.** sexes   **b.** feminist   **c.** quarrel
**d.** nagging   **e.** trousers   **f.** gossip
**g.** flirt   **h.** flattery   **i.** stomach
**j.** beauty
Marry in haste, repent at leisure.

## Page 90   Exercise 5

1. True
2. False – She has had five husbands.
3. False – She controlled them.
4. True
5. True
6. True
7. True
8. False – She didn't spend a lot of money on his funeral.
9. False – She is still interested in love.
10. False – She hasn't been a good wife.

## Tapescript

*My lords, this is the story of my life. Since I was twelve years old, I have had five husbands, all married in church. Some people say you should only marry once but I don't agree. I'm looking forward to the sixth husband. I'm an expert in life and love. You can read about things in books but real knowledge comes from experience. And I've had more experience than any of you.*

*My first three husbands were rich and old. I made them work for me. I spent their money, I stopped them from looking at other women and, before they died, I made them give me all their land and gold. Money is the most important thing in life, I believe. Everything is for sale.*

*But my fourth husband was different. He liked drinking and dancing. He had a girlfriend. That made me angry but I got my revenge! I made him pay for it. I shouted at him, I hit him, I flirted with other men... In the end, he became sick because of me, his terrible wife. I went on a holy pilgrimage to Jerusalem and, when I came back, he was dead. I tell you, I didn't spend a lot of money on his funeral. Why spend money on the dead?*

*I've enjoyed my life. I've had a world of love. And now that I'm older, although I've lost my good looks, I still know how to get a man. Maybe I'll marry one of you!*

## Page 90   Exercise 6

**a.** knowledge
**b.** sale
**c.** on the dead
**d.** world
**e.** good looks/get a man

## Page 91   Exercise 7

**a.** Who hid under the vegetables?
Where did the fox hide?
**b.** Who did Theseus put in the tower?
Where did Theseus put them?
Who put them in the tower?
**c.** Why did they plan the murder?
How many men planned the murder?
**d.** Who suggested a competition?
What did the Host suggest?
**e.** Why did the knight marry the hag?
Who married the knight?

## Page 92   Exercise 8

Open answers.

# PART SIX

## THE FRANKLIN'S TALE

### Page 102   Exercise 1

a. Freedom.
b. Terrible black rocks.
c. No, she didn't.
d. To see a magician.
e. She decided to kill herself.
f. He wanted to be as generous as Arveragus and Aurelius.

### Page 102   Exercise 2

Open answers.

### Page 102   Exercise 3

a. broke out     b. brought about
c. fell out with     d. gave up
e. looked after     f. looked for
g. put forward     h. put off
i. put on     j. set off

a. looked after     b. broke out
c. gave up     d. fell out with
e. brought about     f. put off
g. set off     h. looked for
i. put on     j. put forward

### Page 103   Exercise 4

a. He was the only one she really loved.
b. Jankin.
c. At her grandmother's house.
d. 'If my husband dies, I want you for my next one.'
e. A month.
f. It was a big book with hundreds of stories.

g. Stories about bad women.
h. Three.
i. Because Jankin hit her over the head with the book.
j. He thought that he had killed her.
k. He promised never to hit her again.
l. The book was burnt.
m. Open answer.

### Tapescript

*Let me tell you about my last husband, the only one I truly loved. I was forty and he was twenty. I met him at my grandmother's house. His name was Jankin and he had been a student at Oxford. We went to the fields together while my husband was in London. 'Jankin,' I said, 'if my husband dies, I want you for my next one.'*

*In fact, Jankin helped to carry my husband to his grave. A month later, we got married. At first we were happy. But then he began to beat me. He said that he hated women.*

*The problem was a book. It was a book against women. It was a very big book with hundreds of stories about bad women. Eve, who had given Adam the apple in Paradise. Cleopatra, who had destroyed Mark Antony. Wives who had murdered their husbands.*

*Jankin read this book every night by the fire.*

*At last, I had had enough. I jumped up and tore three pages out of the book. Then I hit him so that he fell backwards into the fire. Immediately, like an angry lion, he picked up the enormous, heavy book. He hit me over the head with it! Bang! That's why I'm deaf in my left ear.*

*Well, I knew what to do. I lay still on*